Dear Myra,
Hope you enjoy t

Rohan

THE SECRETS OF ANGORA:
A MAGICAL DISCOVERY

ROHAN SARMA

Illustrated by Maanas Gopalan Swamy

ABOUT THE AUTHOR

Rohan Sarma, 10, lives in New York City and is passionate about writing fantasy because he can create a world where anything is possible. He was inspired to write this book after reading the Harry Potter series by J.K. Rowling. Writing during the COVID-19 pandemic has been a way for Rohan to step out of reality and dive into a world of his own. He hopes that this book can bring joy and excitement to other kids. Aside from writing, Rohan enjoys playing soccer and board games with his family and cheering on his favorite soccer team Liverpool.

ABOUT THE ILLUSTRATOR

Maanas Gopalan Swamy, 10, lives in Chennai, India and enjoys doodling, reading, and listening to operatic music. He has been practicing Ashtanga yoga for 6 years now and would like to add that he hates peas more than anything in this world!

CONTENTS

ACKNOWLEDGMENTS

I would like to thank my family for encouraging me to write and for being the best listeners in the world. A special thank you to Ms. Nikki Kubeck for teaching me new writing strategies and my mom for helping me edit this book.

CHAPTER ONE

THE FEEL OF MAGIC TO A SIMPLE FOOL

Mrs. Daniel was climbing into her big bed as Mr. Daniel was finishing up his last paper of the week. He had been jumping from call to call for hours but he knew he could not stop. Mrs. Daniel eventually came into his office room just as the clock struck 2 a.m. Her standard comment to him when he stayed up this late was, "That's enough." Mr. Daniel would acknowledge her and go up to bed.

This week, she did not know how much work he had been assigned. He would have to work for 20 hours every day to get his work done for the week.

Mr. and Mrs. Daniel did not have anything particularly special about them, although Mr. Daniel worked in a company called the Jack Company which was famous. He was the lead coder for his company's latest project called the "Scuba Cube." Mrs. Daniel didn't know too many details, but it sounded important and exciting. Mr. Daniel's boss wanted it finished immediately.

Mr. Daniel was a smart looking fellow who had blue eyes, brown hair, and a big nose. He was also very heavy. He usually only wore a suit and a bow tie curling around him which surprisingly did not look so bad. He joined the Jack Company one day five years ago because the owner Jack himself hired him after he met him at a park.

And what do you know? Luck can favor you in many ways. Mr. Daniel was amazing at investments, so he had bought 1% of the company with barely any money and it was now worth approximately $1,000,000,000,000. Well, this might sound like a big number, but keep in mind it's the year 201,927.

Mrs. Daniel was a petite woman and admired Mr. Daniel's dedication to his work. She was curious and smart and volunteered at local charities. Mrs. Daniel loved the color pink but would never wear it. Her attitude towards life was as strong as a ball of fire some people said, but Mrs. Daniel thought that was not really an expression. Now, after five years of marriage, she was ready to be a mother.

Finally, on July 27th in the year 201,929 in an Irish hospital, Mr. and Mrs. Daniel were blessed with a baby boy named Matthew. Matthew had big round eyes, brown hair, and small feet that Mrs. Daniel thought would stay small forever. She thought that he would be the tallest man in the world but be so slow because he had such small feet. Mr. Daniel had to explain what a baby's features were like and what would happen as he grew up. She did not seem that interested in the explanation.

14 Years Later

Matthew was running across the playground like a cheetah running to catch its prey.

"You can't catch me, Adam!" he yelled so his friend could hear. In fact, most people on the playground could hear him. He was leaping from swing to swing until he realized he was in the jungle gym at the far end of the school grounds. He jumped across the top of all the monkey bars, zipping through the air. Matthew was just like Mr. Daniel was as a kid, except a bit more adventurous.

"Try to get me, Adam!" he yelled again to his best friend. This part of the playground was off limits to the students. They were told they should avoid it or risk getting in big trouble. Matthew didn't stop to think about that now. He slid down the pole near him; the pole had a top section made of metal and a lower section made of marble. It was an interesting pole that no one but Matthew had dared to slide down. As Matthew slid down and reached the bottom of the pole, the ground seemed to shift, and he disappeared through the dirt to an underground room. He coughed and wheezed as dirt fell on his face and he could hear people screaming outside on the playground. A little bit of light from above filtered through and to his delight he saw something glittering. It looked like a bunch of fancy stones.

"Wow!" he whispered to himself. "What is this place?" Maybe it wouldn't hurt to take one of the stones home as a souvenir. There were at least a thousand of them. He looked around. How long had they been here? Matthew shoved one into his jacket pocket. Then he climbed up the big pole somehow, dragging himself up. He was panting but managed to reach the top of the jungle gym again. People were staring at him. Then a girl called the teacher over.

"He is back! Now punish him," said a girl named Melissa. She was the teacher's pet. Melissa had brown eyes, blonde hair, and was not Matthew's friend. Melissa was constantly looking for a reason to get Matthew in trouble. Their teacher's name was Ms. Goliath.

Ms. Goliath came rushing to the area. "Thank you, Melissa! It's important to keep me updated on any bad behavior. Ah!" she screamed when she saw where Matthew was standing, covered with dirt. "Matthew, are you okay? Yes - good. Get down right away! You will have to face the consequences of your actions."

Right then Adam joined her. "What's all the fuss about? He went down a pole by mistake! That's it."

Ms. Goliath shook her head, "This area is forbidden to students. You were given instructions very clearly the first week of school. It is dangerous. There was an explosion several years ago and the site is unstable."

Ms. Goliath had a kind looking face and was a good teacher, although she often seemed upset with Matthew. Usually, she was tough on all the children that did not like her favorite students. Also, she didn't think Matthew was a good influence on Adam. It turned out Ms. Goliath was Adam's mom. They looked very similar, both with black hair, green eyes, and brown skin.

After a long lecture from the school Principal about respecting school property, Matthew finally went home. He thought tomorrow he could get more stones. But he was deeply mistaken. He heard an announcement the next morning at school that that pole was completely blocked off and nobody could get near it. The Principal claimed it was for safety issues, but Matthew thought about the stones and guessed there was more to the story. There was something strange lying beneath the playground.

Billions of Miles Away

Wizards and witches were in their classes practicing spells. "Flamero! Flamero!" they yelled, trying to make fire appear in the cauldron. "Try once more class," said Ms. Hopkins. "In four years, each of you will be given important jobs. But first, you guys must crack at least a thousand spells. So do it quick!"

A girl came up to Ms. Hopkins. She had dark skin, black hair, and a yellow shirt. "What happened, Victoria?" asked Ms. Hopkins kindly. Ms. Hopkins' eyes glittered behind her glasses. Her skin looked pale against her black clothing. She also had a necklace on. The necklace was bright blue and looked exactly like water from a clear pond.

"I have done all thousand spells. I have learned everything you have assigned so what do I do now?" asked Victoria.

"If that's the case, you must be quizzed by Terry. If he is impressed, your name goes on the Wall of Honor," replied Ms. Hopkins. "Nobody your age has made it to the Wall of Honor yet."

Victoria exclaimed, "I get to be quizzed by the Principal! That is so cool." Just as she said that an alarm bell sounded.

Ms. Hopkins looked startled. She glanced at the message that appeared on her watch. "All teachers have to see the Principal right now!" she exclaimed. "It must be something urgent. I'll set up your quiz with Terry for next week, okay?" Victoria nodded.

Ms. Hopkins settled herself into the Principal's room and thought that their meeting was off to a slow start. What was all the fuss about? The Principal was about 75 years old and super tall. He was wearing blue, his favorite color, and his white hair was long and straight. He had a square shaped wand with him. There were five or six teachers crowded around him. "I have determined what we need to do. We've had a sign. There is now a path forward."

The teachers looked at each other and gasped. This is the update they had been waiting for.

"Yes! Very exciting. Listen up...We have the information we need to get back our stone. I was shocked when I received an alert on my Non-Magic World projector earlier today. There is a teenager in Ireland who was doing all this cool stuff. Totally fearless and almost flying through the air. I think he has the qualities to be a wizard. But let me get to the point. The precious stones were stored in the basement of the school. Over time, flooding may have caused some stones to wash up from deep down.

"This boy, he spotted the stones and took one. I examined it on the projector and believe it is the exact stone we need. Out of a thousand stones, he got the correct one. That is all we need. And even though he got into trouble with the school, he did not give the stone away."

All the teachers nodded and looked impressed. "Hopkins, I need you to convince him to join our school and bring the stone along. I will give you his address. Off you go!"

CHAPTER TWO

A FLOOD AND A LEAK WITH A BECAUSE AND A SOLUTION

Ms. Hopkins was running with all her might. She started to dive into the ocean. She pinched her nose and yelled, "Fernapolia!" Soon, she teleported herself to Non-Magic World. She arrived flying and saw the side of a big cliff. Again, she screamed, "Fernapolia!" She barely missed the cliff and landed on top of it. Finally, she pointed her wand up at the sky. "Sora!" she yelled. She encountered her own magic bird which had bright feathers but looked very weak.

"Can you please carry me to the top of the hill? This is the only time of the day I can do this spell," Ms. Hopkins asked the bird sweetly. The bird spread his wings and soared high.

Meanwhile, Matthew was lying on his bed, thinking about his day. Adam came to visit him in his room accompanied by Matthew's dad and mom. His parents started to scold him again for the incident at school the day before, but for some reason Matthew kind of liked that. They cared about him.

Mrs. Daniel said in a low and firm voice, "This is horrendous! Your father had to pay $10,000 as a fine for all the repairs on the playground and for your foolish behavior. We are so embarrassed."

But Matthew just smiled. "Nobody was hurt. I was just playing around. And hopefully this will make up for that," he said, as held up his stone for his father and mother to admire. They were speechless for what seemed like several long minutes and then his dad said, "This stone looks really valuable. Where did you find that?"

"It was just lying in the dirt," explained Matthew. "There are thousands of them." Adam reached out to touch the stone. Its edges were like the sharp tip of a rhinoceros' horn and its top shimmered in the evening light. Mr. Daniel was about to speak for a second time when the door to Matthew's room slammed open.

"Oh! I am deeply sorry to disturb your family chat!" said a voice. "Your streets are bigger than my streets. I see you live on, what is it... Oh...um...First Avenue."

Mr. Daniel looked stunned. So did everyone else. "Who are you?" he asked.

"Oh well, I must get out my notecards to... I guess, introduce myself. So, where are these cards? Must have lost them while I was walking upstairs because I remember I had it when I entered your house. I believe I am in Greenland, Iceland, Ireland, or something like that. Anyway, where are those notecards?"

Mrs. Daniel was the first one to find her voice after this. She looked at Ms. Hopkins' kind face and hoped they didn't have anything to be worried about. "How did you get in here? Did we not lock the front door?"

Adam spoke up. "Oh, are you one of those reality show people who is here to surprise everyone with a gift? Maybe you have a big box waiting downstairs with the TV Matthew has been dreaming about."

Ms. Hopkins laughed. "No delivery order for now. I am not from a show. I can tell you who I am once I find my notecards. Just the ordinary ones. The ones that can walk and talk. Not those fancy ones. No! Especially not the ones that can fly." She turned back to see Mrs. Daniel's worried expression.

Mrs. Daniel said, "You have a good imagination but for now let's stick with... the ordinary notecards. Not the ones that can walk or talk, the ones that stay still and—"

She was interrupted mid-speech by the words, "Let me go!" It was a notecard squeaking when Ms. Hopkins pinched it between her fingers and picked it up.

Mrs. Daniel continued, "Was someone speaking? That was probably just my imagination. It looks like you've found your notecards."

Ms. Hopkins started to read what was on it, but it turned out she did not even need the notecards. "So, I'm Ms. Hopkins and I'm a teacher in a school. We believe your son Matthew is actually a wizard. He is very talented, but he has to learn how to control his strength and powers. By which I mean if he hurts even one person, his punishment will be severe. He is also capable of doing amazing things. Matthew needs to come to a boarding school called Angora. Angora has seven classes each year for students of different ages and abilities. One teacher will be assigned per class. I am going to be teaching what is probably the hardest class called 'The Heart of

Magic'.

"Matthew, don't worry, every summer you will be able to see your mom and dad. Unfortunately, you are only allowed to bring regular books, magic books, boxes, magic boxes and a square shaped wand to school."

She paused and turned towards the parents. "Sign this waiver to allow him to attend. Here, take care. I'll be back soon to pick him up. Goodbye!" She left not seeing everyone's shocked expressions.

Matthew tore the waiver into bits and threw it away.

Meanwhile in Magic World

"It's great! He is coming to Magic World. I gave him the waiver," said Ms. Hopkins enthusiastically.

But then the Principal said, "I have been looking at the special cameras Hopkins, and it looks like Matthew tore up the papers."

Ms. Hopkins gasped. "But!" she started and began looking a bit tense.

"You have to persuade the boy – not the parents – and wait for the correct time to strike," he continued. "You see, we have our pieces lined up, so make your trip as long as it needs to be! A few days ought to do it. That will toughen him up a bit. Also, this kid has no idea what Magic World is, so do not use the words 'walking post-it' with him. You have to say something that makes sense to them. Say something funny like a joke. Like, why did the chicken cross the road? To get to the other side. Ha! Ha! See? That's all you have to do to get them on your side, then it is easy."

Ms. Hopkins nodded seriously. "I will definitely try Principal." So once more she made her way to Matthew.

The next day, Adam and Matthew were studying together. "Wow, mate!" said Adam. "I still can't believe you entered a forbidden area and found that cool stone."

Just then, Adam's mom, Ms. Goliath, came into the room. "Time to go, Adam" she said strictly. "I hope you've reminded Matthew that it's never a good idea to disobey rules." The boys said goodbye to each other, and Adam was about to leave when then the worst of the worst happened.

"Matthew," began Ms. Goliath, "Melissa is coming to see you. She begged me for your address. I think she is worried about you and wants to check on you. So be a good boy and welcome her!"

Matthew jumped out of bed, panicked. The last person he wanted to see was Melissa. He was about to tell his parents not to answer the doorbell when he heard it ring. A few minutes later, Mrs. Daniel showed Melissa up to Matthew's room. She pulled on her long blonde hair.

"I have invited some other friends over, Matthew," said Melissa in a sickly-sweet voice. Quietly she said, "I mean, your enemies."

She gave Matthew an evil smile. "We were all so worried about you. This is a big mansion you live in, Matthew. Actually, that is why I wanted to bring my friends here. To play in this big house."

Soon her friends arrived. "Uh-oh" said Matthew, feeling trapped. He was wondering why his mom was letting them all in.

There were three others who entered. One was a boy and two were girls. He recognized all of them. John was always with Melissa and constantly blackmailing Matthew and Adam. Emily played with Melissa in the park and loved insulting him, and Joanne did the same thing as Emily.

"Don't worry. It's not like we're going to stay over or something. Or maybe we will." Melissa smiled her big cheeky smile. Two seconds later the doorbell rang again.

"Who is it now?" wondered Mr. Daniel as opened the door and saw Ms. Hopkins standing there. He slammed the door shut.

"Hey! Let me in, please. All I wanted was to apologize for the trouble I caused yesterday. I was joking. Of course, there is no such thing as magic." She laughed quietly then said, "I actually am a comedian. And I do what comedians do. Do you want to hear a joke? Why did the chicken cross the road? To get to the other side!" she laughed unenthusiastically. "Ha! Ha! Ha!"

Soon, Ms. Hopkins decided to try another tactic with Mr. Daniel. She asked him many questions about his work and remarked, "I think I see why you like finnegans so much."

"It's finance, for the last time" said Mr. Daniel impatiently.

Then Ms. Hopkins said, "Mr. Daniel, I am curious to see what Matthew is doing. Also, where is the stone?"

Astonished, Mr. Daniel asked, "How do you know about the stone?"

"Uh-oh," Ms. Hopkins thought. What would she say now? "Well, I am um... I um..." She stared blankly.

Mr. Daniel waited to see how she would finish her sentence and finally said, "You are a peculiar one. You show up suddenly and know things that are private. Plus, I have guards surrounding the house. How did you get past them this time?"

Ms. Hopkins gulped and said, "Well... I know one of your guards. He told me he spotted something shiny through the window and thinks Matthew is collecting precious stones. He's the one who let me in."

Furious, Mr. Daniel asked, "What was the guard's name?"

Ms. Hopkins used her powers to summon their names and said, "Harry. I don't mean to get him in trouble. You see, I've always admired your house and your family and just wanted a quick peek. Harry has said so many kind things about you, I thought you wouldn't mind if I visited. Also, I have another joke for you. What would you say is odd about this house? Answer: There are no magic post-its!"

Mr. Daniel sighed. He thought for a minute. She was a strange character but seemed harmless. "Since you look tired and are not making any sense, I think the best thing is for you to stay for dinner and head out when you are rested. Plus, you know one of my guards and I fully trust them, so I hope you have only good intentions. Stay for dinner then Harry will escort you back to your home. You can tell him I asked him to."

Ms. Hopkins nodded. She thanked Mr. Daniel for his kindness and went upstairs to find Matthew.

Melissa meanwhile was doing her hair. "I think I will be more stylish with a ponytail, John," she said. "I don't think I want to cut my hair though." She looked at the hair dryer in the bathroom. "A posh hair dryer. Let me wash my hair in the sink so I can use that hair dryer."

Emily and Joanne were on the ground in the bedroom trying to kick Matthew but couldn't quite reach him.

"Do I really have to put up with this?" he asked and a second after he said that he saw the beginning of a giant mess. Melissa had started filling up the tub and was tossing soap and bath bubbles into the water.

"Guys, I changed my mind! Let's create a giant bubble bath. We can wet our feet. That will be so fun." Then she splashed water around. "Join me guys!" she yelled. They all sat on the edge of the tub and splashed their legs. Water was everywhere on the bathroom floor. "Oh, my goodness!" she yelled. "You can't stop us now Matthew because we are the water team! We are unstoppable!"

Matthew was shocked and didn't know what to do. More water spilled onto the bathroom floor. Matthew shut the door, but water came through from the gap under the door. Soon it trickled into the room and down the stairs. Matthew began to panic.

Ms. Hopkins entered Matthew's room right then and saw through the door the kids in the bath making a mess.

"Ayayay!" she yelled in shock. "Mosquo!" she shouted but in the last second realized she did the wrong spell. First the tub flipped over, and the kids fell out and were sprayed by water. Then more water started flooding the room. "Woosh!" the water sounded. The tap stayed on. Ms. Hopkins quickly fixed things.

"No one should know about this! Is that clear?" Ms. Hopkins told the kids fiercely. They nodded vaguely from under the spray of water.

Ms. Hopkins then yelled, "Amorfita!" The water shifted to the side which created a clear path to run on. "Fernapolia!" she yelled and teleported herself out of Matthew's room to the foyer downstairs.

Matthew had seen Hopkins doing all her spells. "Whoa!" he exclaimed and ran down the stairs to find her.

"Dfgsdfgsdf," she shouted with her wand above her head. Matthew was indeed very impressed. But then the bathtub came tumbling down the stairs and he quickly jumped out of the way.

"Watch out!" screamed Matthew but Ms. Hopkins simply

flicked her wand, and the bathtub was in its original place. Then water came sliding out through the upstairs hallway. "S'long!" Ms. Hopkins said. She controlled the water with her wand and threw it onto the fireplace. Everything looked tidy and dry, like it had before Melissa arrived. Matthew was speechless.

"Okay! Let's go join your parents for dinner," said Ms. Hopkins as though nothing strange had happened. Melissa and her friends were crying at this point. They ran out the front door drenched and too scared to even look back.

After dinner, Matthew signaled Ms. Hopkins to follow him into the library. "I wanted to talk to you alone. You know that magic school of yours. I actually... I want to join your school."

Ms. Hopkins smiled her great big smile. "Really?" she asked.

He nodded. "Yes! I want to join."

"Oh, my goodness," said Ms. Hopkins. "Thank you so much! Yes! The Principal will be so proud of me. Wait! I need the stone! Oh no! Oh no! Oh no!" She looked at Matthew. "Do you know where the stone is?"

Matthew looked at her surprised. "How do you know that I have the stone?"

"Magic cameras!" she interrupted. "There is no time to explain! I just need to get the stone for a really important reason. We could save the world. Where is it?"

"Well, it's in my dad's bank locker. He took it there yesterday. He wants to keep it safe while we figure out what it is. The rest of the stones are on school property underground which will be way too risky to get. Do you need it right now?"

Hopkins nodded. "We need the exact stone you found. The one in your dad's bank locker."

"Okay, I want to believe you. We need to sneak into the bank if it's that important. But why should I hand over the stone to you? Are you just here to make money? How do I trust you?"

Ms. Hopkins paused. "You won't understand right now...My world is in danger. But you and the stone are what we have been searching for all this time...Everyone in this world loves money so much they are blind to what is happening around them. We are the ones with our eyes wide open in Magic World. So, if you want a different perspective on life – and defeat some bad guys in the process – now is the time to join me. You have to trust me."

Matthew thought about this. He somehow did trust her. "Okay, when we enter the bank, we will have to disable all the security cameras. And we can't let anybody see us while we're doing it. Can you create a diversion? Maybe make a lot of smoke appear in the bank. Then I can break into my dad's vault, and we can take the stone."

Ms. Hopkins nodded. "That is a good plan," she said. Matthew quickly grabbed a few things and they walked out of the house together trying to melt into the darkness.

CHAPTER THREE

A NEW LIFE LIKE POURING WATER INTO AN EMPTY GLASS

Ms. Hopkins' necklace shimmered in the night sky. She looked down and saw the reflection of every star in the light blue stones.

"Where did you get that necklace?" asked Matthew.

"It is a magic necklace! No real-world necklaces are like this one. It was made from a magic formula called the T-formula. This necklace is what allows me to do magic. If it breaks, I lose my magical abilities and it goes down in a magic chain. That's something you'll be learning about in Angora."

Matthew and Ms. Hopkins noticed a taxi parked across the street. "That's convenient," said Ms. Hopkins. "I was going to teleport us to the bank but it's probably best to act as normal as possible and hop in this taxi." They gave the driver the address to the bank. The taxi driver had brown eyes, brown hair, light skin, and beige colored clothing.

"Do you guys live in that house or were you just visiting?" he asked curiously. He then looked in his rearview mirror and saw Matthew. "Oh, is that Matthew Daniel I see in this car? I've seen pictures of you and your family on the internet." Matthew looked embarrassed and tried to hide in the backseat. He had forgotten that many people around town knew his dad and their family because of his work at the Jack Company.

The driver then looked at Ms. Hopkins. "Who are you?"

"My name is Hopkins, and I am a comedian. What is your name?"

The driver responded "Dean." Suddenly the driver spoke in a different language. He was talking to someone on his phone. Ms. Hopkins frowned. There was something about the driver that she didn't trust. As Matthew watched curiously, she pinched her nose and pulled Matthew's ear.

"Ow! What's that for?" he whined.

"Shh," she responded. "I'm translating what he just said." She listened for a few more minutes until the driver stopped talking. "We're in trouble," she said. "He wants to kidnap you. And he described me as a comedian who is funny looking."

Matthew looked at the GPS by the front seat. "You're right! He is taking us in the opposite direction of the bank! We need to stop. Ms. Hopkins, can you please get us out of this car?"

"Extravagannza!" yelled Ms. Hopkins. Suddenly Dean's seat started to shake.

Ms. Hopkins nodded her head. "Volion" she yelled and the concrete road in front of them lifted. Then, when they were just an inch away from hitting the concrete, they jumped out of the car.

"Phew! That was a close one," said Ms. Hopkins lying on the ground. But she spoke too soon. A few men suddenly appeared and started to pull them away. Before they could react, they were in handcuffs. They soon realized that a police officer was one of the people that carried them. Only one of them was in uniform. The rest seemed to be undercover.

"You know us police officers have eyes in addition to security cameras, right? We were right over there and saw what happened. I'm glad you're both okay. But I want to know who you are and what kind of tricks you are up to!"

Ms. Hopkins looked worried and was trying to figure out what to say. But Matthew had a good idea. "You know the driver of that car is a criminal, right?"

The police officer scratched his head. "Is he?"

"Yes, I'm sure if you look him up, you'll find he has a criminal record. And he was trying to kidnap us. We knew something was strange and when he started to act crazy, we knocked him out. Suddenly there was a loud boom and the concrete in front of us lifted from the impact. We managed to jump out before getting hurt. All we wanted was to get out safely. And I don't know if you recognized me, but I'm Matthew and my dad is Mr. Daniel who works for the Jack Company. He sent me with his - assistant, Ms. Hopkins, to run an errand at the bank. So please let us go or my dad is going to get angry."

The police officer stared at Matthew. He looked at the other police officers and one of them nodded. "Fine!" he said. He removed the handcuffs. Matthew and Ms. Hopkins quickly walked away after giving their thanks. Matthew got a final glimpse of the main police officer. He had blonde hair, a white cap, light skin, brown eyes, and a white T-shirt. Click! He took a mental picture. He suddenly felt numb with fear. For some reason Matthew thought the police officer would start following them.

"We need to run as fast as we can to the bank! I shouldn't have said anything to the police. The bank is officially closed right now. Follow me!" Matthew grabbed Ms. Hopkins' hand as he started to run.

"Gastodian," Hopkins whispered to herself. A hoverboard appeared - an ultra-speedy hoverboard. "Come, get on it with me," she said.

"The bank is straight; right; left; down; up; left; down; up; down; left; left; right," said Matthew looking at his phone and guiding her." She was going really fast now.

"Woohoo!" she yelled. They went on loop after loop and lots of turns. Finally, they made it to the bank.

"Yes! We made it!" yelled Matthew. "And that police officer is way behind us."

Ms. Hopkins leaned the hoverboard on the side of the building. "I'll teleport us into the bank, so the security guards outside won't notice us."

"Okay," said Matthew, "and don't forget we need smoke."

Ms. Hopkins yelled, "Deyu!" Smoke started to get into the bank. They heard a lot of coughing and when everything was covered with smoke, they teleported inside. Matthew knew they had limited time until the smoke would thin out and they would be spotted on the cameras.

"Everything is so foggy. I can't even see where the bank lockers are," said Matthew.

"Really? You came up with this plan and now can't find the locker? It's not like any of us have smoke goggles!"

That gave Matthew an idea. "I always have swim goggles in my backpack for my swim lessons." He dug inside his backpack and found the goggles. "Can you duplicate this please and make sure we can breathe in oxygen too?"

Ms. Hopkins sighed and duplicated the goggles and added some features so they could see and breathe with them on. Suddenly, they noticed the police officer who had been following them come in.

"I'm here to check on any illegal activity," he said loudly to the guards. "Where did this smoke come from? Is there a Matthew Daniel here?"

"Sonare," yelled Ms. Hopkins with her wand pointing at the police officer. He was flung against the wall and couldn't move. Matthew had reached the room with the lockers in the meantime and typed in the letters LEINAD on the lock pad, just as he had observed his dad doing the last time they had visited. It clicked open and he took out the stone.

"Now teleport us out of here!" yelled Matthew. He could hear footsteps near them.

"I can't teleport us right now! My powers seem to have weakened. We need to get to the special hoverboard outside."

"Okay! Let's go!" Matthew started to walk towards the exit. But then all the smoke disappeared, and the alarm started blaring. The bank went on full lockdown. One by one, police officers came in.

"Okay! You—" someone began but Ms. Hopkins interrupted it with, "Sheckti!"

All the police officers lined up in a single file and were pushed to the ground, unable to move. Matthew noticed a button by the bank manager's desk and tried pressing it. They heard a click and realized the front door was now open. The two quickly exited the bank and got on the special hoverboard. Ms. Hopkins touched her necklace and teleported them to Magic World.

The police officers finally got up and were dazed. They would have a lot of explaining to do to their boss, Ms. Goliath.

* * *

Ms. Hopkins and Matthew landed in Magic World. It was a different feeling the second Matthew landed. He was finally there! He was gone from Earth. He saw all the trees had one branch that touched the ground. It was like a slide built into every tree.

"It's a beauty, isn't it?" said Ms. Hopkins. "Oh, we need to get you a wand before you go anywhere."

Matthew nodded. "This is paradise. I can't wait to explore Magic World." But then Mrs. Hopkins got a call on her special phone. The person on the end was screaming so she had to hold the phone away from her ear.

"Hopkins! Come to my room right now! We need to talk

about what happened in Non-Magic World!"

Ms. Hopkins gave Matthew a nervous smile and ran to the Principal's office. For a few seconds, the Principal and Ms. Hopkins stared at each other and did not speak. Finally, the Principal shared his thoughts.

"Have you thought about all the trouble you have caused us? Involving innocent people and bringing attention to Matthew and yourself. People on Earth are after us now. You could have just teleported back with the kid, and I would have helped you out. Instead, you risked his life! His parents don't even know you have left Earth with him."

Ms. Hopkins gave a shout. "I am sorry Terry! I should have been more aware of what I was doing. Our plan went wrong from the minute we got into the taxi. I didn't know what else to do. Please give me some sympathy!"

The Principal sighed. "If I must."

"Thank you. I know you will help me fix everything."

The Principal sighed again. He seemed calmer now. "At least you brought back the boy and the stone. Now please get Matthew a wand!" He escorted Ms. Hopkins out of his office.

"We have to pick up a wand for you," Ms. Hopkins said to Matthew when she returned. "We really have to do it right now."

They went to a store called "The Arnold Wand Shop." There was a skinny man with a big smile on his face when they entered. He had blue eyes, brown hair, and a bright blue shirt. "Hello! You are the new kid I was expecting. Ms. Hopkins is welcome to watch you find your wand if she wants."

Ms. Hopkins nodded her head.

"Good!" he said. "You know, the start of being a wizard is entertaining to watch." He paused. "I am Mr. Arnold. So, what design do you want? And what length do you want your wand to be? Big, small, or medium?"

Matthew thought for a second. He would have this wand for his whole life so it would be super important to choose the right one. "I want to have a wand with ninjas on it. I want it to be medium sized and the ninjas should have grey hats," he finally said confidently.

"Excellent choice. Please wait for 30 minutes and I will have your wand ready. Have a seat."

Matthew was excited to see his wand being made. "Now I only have to mix it with the Z-formula," said Mr. Arnold. He closed his eyes and put a purple liquid on the ninja wand. But at the last second, he gulped. "Kid! This isn't going to work out. Sorry but you have to choose a different design."

Matthew looked confused. "Why?" he asked Mr. Arnold.

"You see Matthew, I thought you chose a design that no one has ever chosen yet, except, guess what?" Matthew shook his head meaning he did not know. "The Principal of Angora. His wand has ninjas on it. I totally forgot - my dad gave the wand to him. It is just an amazing work of art. But I don't know the formula for the serum on it, that is the problem. So, it is a bit challenging. The ninja wand is made from a special formula that does not require the Z dose. Sorry, but I cannot make it for you. I think that you deserve the wand you chose. It's amazing. Ah!"

He then smiled and said, "Come on! Choose your new wand."

Matthew thought and then said, "I either have the ninja wand, or I leave!"

"Matthew!" yelled Ms. Hopkins.

"No! It's quite all right. I know you're upset. I have a wand with a heart and pink daisies!" said Mr. Arnold, hoping this would please him.

"Never! Just give me a different good wand please," was Matthew's response.

"Okay! I can give you a wand with unicorns!" Matthew slammed his fists against a wall and felt like there was smoke coming out of his ears. Ms. Hopkins did not want things to get worse, so she just thanked him and examined the wand.

"10 inches long!" she murmured as they were leaving the shop. "This is good."

Matthew just shook his head. He seemed to be stuck with a wand that was nothing close to his first choice. This was not a good start. But he perked up when he saw the school. "Wow," he whispered, pushing the disappointment with the wand to the back of his head.

The school was the biggest building he had ever seen. It was as big as a hundred dinosaurs and had many colors. The front of the school was as yellow as a school bus and the sky right above was black and dark. There was a flag that said 'ANGORA' and a bridge with people who were pointing their wands at each other. A tree stood majestic at one end of the school. He was about to walk into Angora when Ms. Hopkins stopped him.

"No! Don't go in there! School starts tomorrow! Summer camp ends today."

"Summer camp is still going on? Isn't it almost midnight now?" Matthew was confused.

"There is a bit more homework here than in regular schools. It is very hard. Hm..I should check on Victoria."

Matthew stopped. "Who is Victoria?" he asked.

"Long story!" she said. "Well, I think we'd better get going. Tomorrow will be a special day because you will find out what group you go into. Group A, B, C, D, E, F, G, H, I, and J. The Principal will sort you. You are in Grade 9. Anyway, I am going to find you a room where you will stay for the night. We will sort out a student room for you tomorrow. Just don't move."

Matthew did as Ms. Hopkins said. He waited outside. Then a boy his age came up to him. He had brown eyes, light skin, black hair, and a yellow T-shirt.

"Hi! My name is Tom! Who are you?"

Matthew looked at him. "I am Matthew! I am new to this school. I just got here."

Tom looked confused. "Where did you study before? This is the only magic school around."

"Oh! I uh... I went to a normal school. You know...school for people that do not have powers."

Tom looked even more confused now. Matthew was eager to ask Tom a question, but Tom said something before Matthew could speak up. It was a bit annoying, but he needed friends if he wanted to survive this school year.

"A school where no one is a wizard or witch? Why didn't you just go to this school?"

Matthew sighed. "My mum and dad are not wizards or witches. I am from Ireland, but I turned out to be a wizard. I think...Where do you live?"

Tom started talking fast. "I live with my mom in a nearby village. She's a news reporter. I'm here as a summer school kid. I'm not sure I'm going to stay for the year. As a new kid, you will have a lot of work to do. Even the kids in summer camp stay up late. So, um... Why are you up this late? I mean, you have the right to ask me the same question, but I am asking you first."

Matthew's head was spinning. "Ms. Hopkins picked me up from my family and brought me here. We arrived a short time ago. Who brought you here?"

"My mom brought me here two months ago. Her job keeps her really busy, and she travels a lot. Which is why I'm thinking of staying back here for 9th grade."

Matthew nodded. "Well, I hope that your mom stays safe traveling around this... Magic World."

"Thanks!" Tom said gratefully, "I hope you have a good time in Angora."

CHAPTER FOUR

A DAY OF WORK AND A TEMPTATION TO LIE DOWN

Ms. Hopkins sat down next to Ms. Teach in the teachers' lounge.

"Another visit to Earth?" Ms. Teach asked.

"The last one!" said Ms. Hopkins. "I am done running around for the Principal. On top of that, I have to listen to you, too. I quit. It is too much work."

Ms. Teach shook her head. "But it's the Principal who is giving you the hard work! I just want you on my side."

Ms. Hopkins' eyes darted towards Ms. Teach. "You won't dare speak of the Principal like that! It's one thing for me to complain...You've said enough bad things about him."

Ms. Teach pleaded with her. "Hopkins! Think of all the progress we made together. Think of the ways we can improve the school with the Principal out of the way—"

"Well, looks like you will be on your own since I am done with you," Ms. Hopkins interrupted.

"You're involved already, and you know the consequences if the Principal finds out. We have to keep this project a secret. You must stay on my side in order for this to work. If you leave now, bad things will happen, and it will all be your fault. I have scheduled an appointment with Ms. Ivan tomorrow as part of the plan. So, if you will excuse me, I am off to bed. Goodnight." Ms. Teach ended her speech dramatically by rushing out of the room.

Ms. Hopkins sighed deeply and was anxious about what she had gotten herself into. She was still thinking about her situation when she walked back to her room and forgot about Matthew until the next morning. She woke up and suddenly remembered him and exclaimed, "Oh man!"

She walked straight outside and checked every single spot she could think of. Matthew, meanwhile, woke up startled in the patch of grass where he had fallen asleep. He thought that this was just a dream. Then he saw kids entering the school and joined them. This was going to be an interesting morning.

Down the hall, Ms. Teach was in a meeting with Ms. Ivan. Ms. Teach started talking. "I am going to host a few more of these meetings but this is my first one. I wanted to have a discussion with you about your job. Oh, and – achoo!"

Ms. Teach pretended to sneeze but instead made all security cameras go wrong by raising her wand.

Ms. Ivan eyed Ms. Teach suspiciously. "Why exactly did you call this meeting?"

Ms. Teach smiled. "I have a job that I want you to know about. I have been plotting this for many years and you are key to making it happen. Don't you ever feel that Principal Terry has far too much power? He can fire you or make you his puppet just by snapping his fingers, but if you are by my side, I am not going to let that happen. We will be unstoppable. Imagine taking over the entire school and shaping the education of these students the way we want. We will be the most powerful women around. It will be fun," she said with an evil smile. "We will first take over the Principal's job, then we will take over the school. Don't worry, the children won't be harmed."

Ms. Ivan sounded alarmed by this. "But I would never want to go against the Principal! I like him and think he's doing a good job. And I don't want to take over the school. I mean, this is the only wizard and witch school in Magic World. No! I am not going to agree to this." She looked up at the security camera hoping someone could see and hear their conversation. But, of course, the security cameras were no longer working.

"Sorry, then I have no choice but to do this now!" Ms. Teach yelled. "Calerfo, Mostuisco!"

Suddenly Ms. Ivan was trapped in a chest in the corner of her room. She was helpless.

"Don't worry! You'll have a steady supply of food and water. Just tell me if you want to join my side and get the special job!" said Ms. Teach cheerfully as she teleported back to her room.

Meanwhile, after about another ten minutes of searching, Ms. Hopkins found Matthew in a classroom on the first floor. "Good school, isn't it?" she said casually. Matthew was so surprised that he jumped up from his chair.

"Oh! Did not mean to surprise you there," she said. "Sorry

about last night. Glad you found your way! The group sorting is going to happen in the next hour."

Then Matthew saw Tom enter the school. "Hi!" said Tom.

"Hi, Tom! It looks like you decided to stay back. Are you ready for the sorting groups?" asked Matthew, glad to see a familiar face.

"More than ready! I changed into the fanciest clothes my mom got me." He indeed did look very nice. He had a white T-shirt with black and white checks on it as though people were just about to play a chess game on that shirt. His shoes were completely black with long laces. Tom's wand was long with orange alligator drawings on it.

Soon after, they sat down to be sorted. Everyone sat up straight when they saw the Principal.

"Hello, everyone! Attention!" he yelled. "This group is specifically for kids in 9th grade. 9th grade as we know is high school. High school means a lot more work. Before I announce who is going to which group, I would like to recognize a special student who has gotten perfect scores on all her homework assignments and tests over the years. Victoria Falls! Come on up!"

Victoria walked up to the Principal.

"Nerdy girl!" Tom whispered to Matthew. "She thinks she's the smartest one in class! But this year I will challenge her and beat her."

Then the Principal said, "Now the sorting begins. In the sorting there will be groups A,B,C,D,E,F,G,H,I and J. A stands for

Advanced! They are a very smart group. B stands for Bravery. C stands for Core! They are good at fighting. D stands for Doodlers. These are students who have great potential but are easily distracted. E stands for Epic. They have accomplished most things a wizard needs to accomplish. F is Fraud. The Frauds are good at finding shortcuts to accomplish their goals. G stands for Gain. That one is a little confusing, but it means they will never ever show mercy or sympathy to others and are interested in their own gains. They will fight until they win. H stands for Hornet. They are the ones that will come after you when they get a good angle to bite you. Oh! They will hurt. I stands for Igloo. That means that when someone attacks, they will stand still and fight back hard! But that is only *if* you annoy them. Finally, J stands for Joker. They are the people that will cause trouble in class.

"Now, these groups are just based on the notes we have taken over the last few years. There are a lot of people in each group but Epic only has 3 people! As we know, the group names are based on your personality but don't let that define you. Do not get sad if you are in what is considered a bad group. And do not brag if you are assigned to a good group, because that does not mean that you are amazing. We picked these groups to show you that the real world has people with good qualities and bad qualities. You can learn a lot from each other and improve your skills, and you'll see that people who are meant to be good can do bad things. Those who we think have bad qualities can also do a lot of good."

Then he stopped and said, "Now, let me say the names

aloud. Group A has Dugbort, Cammas, Entfan, Sectron, Gidion, Desiduan, Mulimy, Mulimy's mother? Um... I think that was a wrong name. Delete that.

"Anyway, Group A also has Croni, Dawn Golyma, Sasha, and Bob. Group B has 12 people. Their names are written in wizard languages so I will just say them in those languages. FU, HJI, HKO, KJN, JHG, MNB, LKJ, UGV, MSJ, IJH, HHH, MMM. The C and D groups are apparently in another building so let me announce group E next. Victoria! We know she's a star student. Tom! The only one that was in the Advanced Magic class this summer. And Matthew Daniel! Let's welcome him, he's a new student."

Everyone clapped as Matthew and Tom grinned. The rest of the announcements happened quickly. The boys ran out of the room together to celebrate. But there were a few people whispering. "Why was he chosen?"

"A poor winner, he is, if you have ever heard of that. But I guess that means the rest of us play the role of the poor losers then."

A group of students walked towards Matthew and Tom. "Hello! You think you're so cool, don't you? You don't even know a single spell," a boy yelled close to Matthew's and Tom's ears.

"Hey! What was that for!" Tom exclaimed.

"I CAN'T HEAR YOU! SPEAK UP!" screamed the bully again.

"Let's run!" Matthew whispered to Tom. But they ran too fast around the corner and bumped into Ms. Teach out in the hallway.

"Oh! Hello! Sorry about that," said Tom.

Ms. Teach gave them a big smile. A good and evil smile all at once. "I actually want to talk to you both. Everyone is wondering why you got sorted into group E." She lowered her voice. "It's not because Principal Terry thinks you're smart. It's because he wants to keep an eye on you in a small class. Epic students? No! You're not going to last in this school very long, and..." She crouched down and started whispering. They could not make out what she was saying. It is probably a magic language Matthew thought to himself. He was surprised he could make out a few words.

"Security cameras...Traitor Hopkins. Well, at least no one is suspicious of me," were the only words he could make out.

"Strange. Come on! Let's go!" Matthew yelled. He and Tom ran as fast as they could.

The Next Morning

Victoria, Tom, and Matthew were sitting in a triangle. "I think our group E will talk about the Magic Sectors. It doesn't matter that you are new here, Matthew. You will understand it at the same level as Tom. He just got here this summer. And they're going to give us a beginning of the year test! It's Ms. Teach's test. They are the hardest because they don't always make sense. Last year, I was so sure I got all the questions right! Even the Principal said so, but I got a C. It was so sad. Luckily, it didn't go on my official record. Maybe she wants more work to be shown? Maybe she wants to have the 11th recording of secron! Maybe she—"

"Is evil!" Matthew finished.

"Ha!" laughed Victoria. "None of our teachers are evil. Crazy at times, but not evil."

Tom shook his head. "She was acting very strange yesterday. She said something about security cameras, we think. Matthew heard her say that when she thought we couldn't understand her."

Victoria looked puzzled. "Why would she mention the security cameras?" she asked.

Tom hesitated and said, "I don't know. But she basically told us we wouldn't last long at the school. She sounded threatening!"

Victoria stared at them. "This is not a prank, is it?" she asked. They shook their heads. "That is disturbing."

Just then Ms. Hopkins came in. "You guys have class right now! What are you doing here sitting around?"

Victoria looked worried. "Ms. Hopkins, we need to tell you something. You know Ms. Teach well, right? Matthew and Tom had a strange encounter with her. She seemed to threaten them. We really like you Ms. Hopkins and trust you. But we think something bad is going on."

Ms. Hopkins turned white.

"Also, why did she call you a traitor?" Tom spoke up.

Ms. Hopkins gulped. "I—"

"Will you tell them or shall I, Hopkins," said a familiar voice. It was Ms. Teach. "I heard what the kids are saying about me." She looked sternly into their eyes. "Disrespecting a teacher and spreading rumors is considered a crime at this school. But you do not have to worry dears, I am not a tattletale," she finished sweetly.

Victoria had to force herself not to respond with a rude comment.

Ms. Hopkins shook her head. "Children," she said quietly. "I'll handle this. Off to class now."

As the kids walked into class, Ms. Teach stared at Ms. Hopkins. "I'm keeping an eye on you, Hopkins. And you better keep an eye on those kids. I don't want any trouble." With those words, she walked away.

* * *

Meanwhile in Ireland, Mr. Daniel was busy thinking, "What if that lady who calls herself Ms. Hopkins has kidnapped Matthew? The security camera caught them leaving together. What if she was serious about taking Matthew to some magic school. Oh, no! I can't believe I trusted her."

Mrs. Daniel was terribly upset herself but went to comfort him. "We're going to get him back, don't worry." Then they noticed a text message on their phones. "Matthew must have managed to keep his phone with him," said Mrs. Daniel, relieved.

The text was from an unknown number. The message read, "I am fine. Sorry I left without talking to you. I needed to see Magic World for myself. It is great! How are you doing? By the way, we had to take the special stone from dad's bank locker. Also, I helped myself to one of the Scuba Cubes that dad brought back from the office. I know he was testing the communication range and guess what? I'm able to use it to send this message from Magic World."

He also had a video of himself smiling.

"There he is. I can't believe he ran off with a stranger. Oh, no! You think maybe she brainwashed him?" asked Mr. Daniel. But Mrs. Daniel wasn't listening. She had already come up with a plan. "So that's Magic World! Now we know what it looks like. We need to bring Matthew back home. It's time we invoke the best hacker and engineer in the world. Mr. Brown!" She smiled and Mr. Daniel did the same.

* * *

Matthew went into the hallway outside class with Victoria and Tom. "Wow!" he said. All the walls were made of a shiny metal that he had never seen before. They were so bright that the effect was like small goldfish lighting up a big river.

"Wow!" he said a second time. As he stood admiring the hallways, Matthew couldn't help thinking that maybe he was meant to go to this school. They entered their first class and were met with warm welcomes from the teacher. The teacher had brown hair, big eyes like Matthew, dark skin and was short. The room had books piled from top to bottom. It seemed like a trillion books were crammed into a small area of the room.

"Hello! I am Mr. Simon. I am going to teach you the Night of Magic Squares class this year. For the first one or two classes, I will not be teaching you spells, but will assign homework to review material from last year."

Matthew sighed with relief. He was worried he wouldn't understand anything in class.

"In this class, we will start with a test to see how much you know. First, I must ask for all your names. I know Victoria and Tom, but I do not know who my third student is. What is your name?"

"Matthew," he replied immediately.

"Matthew! The new kid. Do your best on the exam." This did not help Matthew relax at all. Then Mr. Simon said, "Learning time." He pulled out his book. "Okay! I must set up chemical squares for us to mix. We must mix it up at the right time. Let me tell you a little about the chemicals that I will be using. Chemical X, Chemical Y, and Chemical Z, three chemicals that have evolved over time. They started out as little creepers on the Magic Wall, but now have become powders that can help us in our everyday life."

Mr. Simon smiled. They all put the formulas in, but Matthew was so nervous his hands kept shaking. This was all so new to him.

"So, Victoria, it seems like every Chemical has an alphabet assigned to its name, right?" asked Matthew.

Victoria looked confused. "What's an alphabet?" she asked.

Matthew was puzzled that the smartest girl in school was asking about alphabets. "You know," he said in a sing-song voice. "A, B, C, D, E, F, G...Just like the classes we got sorted into."

"Those are part of the letter set! 1, A, 2, B, 3, C, 4, D. That's the letter set."

Matthew shook his head. "You're mixing numbers and alphabets!" But before he could clarify what he meant, Mr. Simon told them to be quiet.

The school bell rang soon, and next they went to the Heart

of Magic class with Ms. Hopkins. The class had a mix of students from groups A, B, and E. Ms. Hopkins seemed calmer now. She was repeating a few jokes that she learned from trying to be a comedian when she met the Daniels. The class started off with a spell called, "Flamero!" which would make fire go into a cauldron. Most people that attended summer camp knew the spell. They practiced for 30 minutes, and Matthew found it hard to even move his wand for that spell. Then they learned something that Matthew could actually understand. They learned about The Heart of Magic.

"The Heart of Magic is a concept where magic is attached to you. For example, my heart of magic is my mom and dad. They have guided me through every single step of my magic. But there is one thing. If your attachments fall, your magic will never be performed well!" She looked at all of them sternly.

Then she said, "When my mom died, my powers became weaker. If my dad dies, my attachments become weaker. When both my parents die, I am powerless." She paused and looked closely at the children.

"There is also something called the attachment chain which is very complex. We will be learning more about it in the following weeks, but these are the basics. You are born with an attachment which can be a person or persons or an object. But that does not mean they have to be a wizard or witch. They might be someone who doesn't know magic but who appreciates it.

"Now, this is the complex part. If my mom and dad lose whatever their attachment is, it will go down one cycle or one chain.

Then I also lose my magic since they lost their magic. Once my parents' attachment is gone, then my attachment is also gone, and we cannot perform magic."

Then one student asked, "How do you know what your attachment is? And is there a way of getting your magic back if you lose it?"

Ms. Hopkins sighed. "These are good but complicated questions. If you go to the Magic Wall, it will reveal your attachment to you because energy waves will travel from the wall to your brain. In terms of whether you can get your magic back if you lose it...We are still trying to understand if this is possible. Some wizards and witches do regain their magic but we're not entirely sure why. Perhaps they are given a new attachment, but we haven't been able to confirm this."

The students left the class both confused and excited. It was now time for lunch.

"Um... Is it fair to ask what food you typically eat here?" asked Matthew. "I'm starving." He looked at the salad bar and saw all the foods had purple leaves with what looked like purple guacamole. This did not look appealing to Matthew.

"Oh, have you not tried these foods? You need to have a taste for magical and non-magical foods. Believe it or not, it is actually very yummy," said Tom.

"Do you want to go to the Spice Station or the Magic Pizza

Station?" asked Victoria.

"Magic Pizza Station," said Matthew instantly. They walked to the pizza bar and Matthew saw green pizza with purple guacamole on top. He turned to Tom and shook his head, but when he turned back, the pizza had his name MATTHEW on it spelled with his favorite toppings, and a side of bread sticks.

"Yes!" he exclaimed as his grabbed a plate.

After lunch they entered a Science Magic class the students had shortened to Science Mag. The whole grade had to attend this class. Matthew could see all kinds of faces. Happy, angry, sad, and excited. They all looked up when Ms. Hopkins entered the room.

"Hello, class! I'm your substitute teacher today. Welcome to the Science Mag class. Today we will be learning how to turn a live bee into a stuffed animal bee using both science and magic. We will be using potions and formulas but no wands in this class. I promise, the bees won't feel a thing. In fact, I'll also show you how to turn them back into live bees." Ms. Hopkins started to demonstrate what to do, and the class got to work.

After this, they went to the next class, Boo Boo Magic, taught by Ms. Teach.

"I will be teaching the class how to find a needle in a haystack in less than a second," she said and laughed at their surprised faces. "We will use an advanced spell called WDLT. You won't find this in any spell books since I came up with it and am the only one who knows it."

"Why are you the only one who knows it?" asked Victoria.

45

"I thought teachers were supposed to share any new spells as soon as they created them."

"Why?" Ms. Teach repeated. She looked uncomfortable. "Sometimes we forget to report a new spell," she said and turned her back to them to look at the ingredients on the table.

Matthew was listening carefully and felt something was not right. He signaled to Tom who nodded that something was off.

Victoria suddenly stood up and said, "Wait – I know why WDLT sounds so familiar. I overheard Principal Terry talking to Ms. Hopkins about it. He was upset because someone had written that on the wall of his office... It stands for We Don't Like Terry."

The other students looked confused. Was this a coincidence? Or was Ms. Teach sharing a spell that would set them against the Principal?

Ms. Teach looked around the room nervously. She blinked her eyes obviously making class bell ring. "We're out of time - class is over! Homework is to practice this spell. I've written the instructions on the blackboard. Make a recording and send it to me. Bye!" She left before anyone else could react.

Matthew, Tom, and Victoria went back to group E room to discuss things.

"That was strange. I know she's lying but I don't know why. I think she has something against the Principal. Well, she ended class early, so I guess I bought us an hour of free time with all my questions!" said Victoria.

"Impressive!" replied Matthew. "You're really observant.

And thank you for getting us that extra free time."

Victoria looked at all her homework assignments and frowned. "Ms. Hopkins' homework is so easy but writing out the spells is hard work. But at least her video about the Heart of Magic is simple." Then she looked at their Science Mag homework. "Okay. Done!" she said happily. Finally, she looked at their 2nd sheet of Boo Boo Magic work. "Oh, no! Not even Ms. Teach can solve this. It's so hard!"

Matthew knew he would not be able to do any of the homework, so he giggled. "I don't know any of this. I'm just going to relax and take a nap."

But Victoria stopped him. "You are in group E! You are supposed to be one of the smartest students in the grade. If you do not do something as simple as your homework, the Principal's feelings about you may change."

Matthew sighed, "It was all a mistake. I wasn't even meant to be put into group E. Only a little while ago I saw that magic was real, and now I am expected to be among the top in the grade?"

"At least learn the concepts!" Victoria begged.

Matthew sighed. "Fine! But I might go to sleep if it is too boring." He started to look through a few of Victoria's formula books.

* * *

A little while later, the three of them went back to the Night of Magic Squares for their 8 to 9 p.m. class. Matthew was yawning like crazy, and they were supposed to have the energy to take a test.

47

"Okay. Class E, take your test!" yelled Mr. Simon. "3-2-1 GO! GO! GO!"

The first question was, "What is the X-formula + Y-formula + Z-formula to the second alpha?" Matthew skipped these first few questions until he had an idea. He smiled. "Mr. Simon, I am thirsty! Can I—"

"Quiet!" Mr. Simon interrupted. "No talking, no moving."

Matthew now had a backup plan. "Um... Mr. Simon, it looks like you have lots of potions. I see 24 of them!"

Mr. Simon was about to tell him to be quiet again but then gasped. "Wait! Did you say 24? I'm supposed to have 25 of them." He looked around. "Sneaky kids are always trying to run off with my best potions."

Matthew nodded. "I'm pretty sure I heard someone showing off your potion during our evening break. I don't know his name...I think he's in Group B."

Mr. Simon started breathing hard. "Continue your test but I am going to look around and get my potion back."

He left and Matthew chuckled. This was exactly what he had planned. Victoria had told Matthew how attached Mr. Simon was to his potions. He knew that Mr. Simon was supposed to have 25 potions and had seen one fallen on the ground behind the bookshelf.

"What was that all about?" asked Victoria. "Why were you trying to get him out of the room?"

"Oh," Matthew said. "I thought that was obvious. Well, I can't do any of the questions on this test. I would rather learn more about Ms. Teach, Ms. Hopkins, and Ms. Ivan. This room probably has all the books I need but Mr. Simon seems to always keep it locked. I am going to get some information. I know exactly where the section on teachers is. Do you want to look with me?"

Tom jumped to his feet, but Matthew suddenly felt guilty. "I don't want to ruin things for the two of you though. You should probably focus on the test. I'm going to fail this test anyway so I may as well look."

Matthew pulled out his Scuba Cube. "I can take pictures—"

Victoria laughed. "You can't use your phone to take pictures or scan papers! These are magic papers. If anything besides a wizard or witch's wand is in close range with those papers, an alarm will sound. The only way to get away with this is to bring the book to the Epic room which we are a million percent not doing."

"Well, let's vote on it," said Tom who had been quietly listening.

Just then they heard the door unlocking. "Get back to your seat!" hissed Victoria to Matthew.

They had just enough time to put the book into Victoria's magic box (which is like a backpack that can fit an infinite number of things and is invisible to everyone but the owner). Mr. Simon caught Matthew running to sit on his chair and eyed him suspiciously.

"I believe you are all done with your tests?" said Mr. Simon. "And I certainly hope there was no discussion about the answers." He seemed to be in a bad mood.

Matthew responded, "I still want to answer the last two questions. May I please answer them?" he asked sweetly.

Mr. Simon sighed. "Go ahead. Answer the last two questions." He looked curiously at his paper. "How many questions have you answered so far?"

"Um..." Matthew hesitated.

"Exactly!" said Simon. "I think you are just playing around with me. Now hand in your tests."

"Well, as I said I wanted to fin—"

"Hand in your tests!" Mr. Simon raised his voice and looked upset. They quietly handed in all their test sheets and walked out.

"I'm definitely off to a terrible start in this class, thanks to you," grumbled Tom to Matthew. "I could have answered most of the questions if I weren't so distracted."

Victoria looked thoughtful. "If all of us did really badly, I think it will be difficult for Mr. Simon to share those grades with the Principal. Besides, it's the first test of the year. He's supposed to teach us new things and then test us again. So, let's not worry about grades right now." Still, Victoria was frustrated. And she grew angry when she saw Matthew pulling out his Scuba Cube to text his parents. She grabbed it from him.

"Argh!" she yelled and threw his Scuba Cube in the trash. Victoria just meant to shock him, but she had forgotten this was no ordinary trash can. Matthew's eyes widened as he looked inside. He saw his device go down an infinitely long slide and disappear into darkness.

CHAPTER FIVE

SKETCHY MOVEMENTS & TECHNICAL DIFFICULTIES

The Scuba Cube that was thrown in the trash made its way into the junkyard. A teacher called Mr. Fire came into the Principal's office.

"An unidentified object came to our junkyard. On the back it says Matthew, the name of the new kid. Well, at least I hope he learned that you can't bring anything besides books, boxes, and a wand to Angora. Do you think you should tell the boy what he did was unacceptable and—"?

The Principal shook his head. He had never seen this type of device before, but he thought it looked like a thin version of a book. "No! The boy is not from our land. He just needs time to adjust into this life."

Mr. Fire nodded. "Okay! I will bring this phone thing with me and give it back to him soon." The Principal agreed that was a good idea.

* * *

Back in Ireland, Mr. and Mrs. Daniel requested Brown to help them. Brown had brown skin as dark as chocolate, bright blue eyes and had yellow pants. Mr. and Mrs. Daniel bowed down to him. They would do anything to get their Matthew back.

"Wait! Wait! Wait! You are saying I need to hack into some place called Magic World? And you're giving me no clue on where it is? I am sorry but I don't really believe in Magic World. I mean—"

But Mrs. Daniel looked at him furiously. "This Magic World is probably going to wage war on us soon. Earth will fall unless we act!" she lied. Mr. Daniel nodded. They had to convince Brown to help them.

"And think of all the treasures. What if they make the iPhone version 100,000,000 that can let you teleport to the person you are calling or texting?"

Brown looked amazed. "Okay! I am doing this!" he yelled.

Mr. Daniel gave him his Scuba Cube so he could see pictures of Magic World. "All we need is a few more pictures. And maybe some more messages from Matthew to give us more information on this place."

Just as they said that they heard a beep on their phone and got several pictures of Magic World. They assumed it was from Matthew, but it was actually Mr. Fire who had accidently put those photos in a file and sent it to the last contact on his list. Mr. Daniel grinned and was as happy as a clam.

* * *

Matthew, Victoria, and Tom went to class the next day with Mr. Simon. Mr. Simon went through the day's schedule. "You have your Terrain Class with Mr. Fire. That's a new class that we did not have yesterday, Matthew. And, of course, we have your favorite class, Tom - the Wizard Animals class."

Tom smiled. "Yes!" he applauded.

Mr. Simon then opened a book. "Now, take out Book of Nocturnal Magic Animals from your bag, Matthew. Hopkins should have given you your copy."

When Matthew shook his head Mr. Simon said, "Fine. Take my copy instead for now." Matthew was about to reach for the book, but Victoria jumped in.

"Actually, that wouldn't work Mr. Simon. Remember, we need to bring our animals to life so we can observe them and feed them. Matthew needs his own copy of the book to do that."

"I have an idea!" added Tom. "The three of us will find Ms. Hopkins right now and bring the book back. Matthew doesn't know the school well enough yet. If we go together, we'll be quick."

Mr. Simon sighed. "Why waste our class time? You are trying something tricky and think I'm not smart enough to find out."

"What?" Tom shouted a little too loudly. He was trying to sound innocent but probably sounded like a screaming gorilla pounding his chest. "Do you think Matthew, a new kid, would go wandering around trying to misbehave? He would be most scared of the consequences of breaking the rules. So please just let us get the books from Ms. Hopkins."

"I really wish the security cameras were still on," remarked Mr. Simon. "Terry is still trying to fix them. But go! Get the book and be back immediately." They went out. Mr. Simon grunted. "I somehow don't trust those kids."

Tom, Matthew, and Victoria checked in the teachers' lounge, cafeteria and finally went up to Ms. Hopkins' apartment. They knocked and waited then tried the front door. It was open. But Ms. Hopkins seemed to be still sleeping in her bedroom. They could hear her snoring.

"Are you sure Ms. Hopkins has the book?" Tom whispered to Victoria but then his question was answered. There was a box set aside, right by her bedroom door that said, "Matthew's books."

"That must be it," said Victoria. Then Matthew and Tom noticed something unusual for Ms. Hopkins. There was an alarm set on a table outside her bedroom for 10 a.m.

"I think she wants to sleep in," whispered Tom. They picked up the box and walked quietly back to class.

Mr. Simon was staring at them suspiciously when they got back.

"You took that long just to retrieve a book? Ugh! Let us start learning about the W-Formula before I get too mad at you. The W-Formula is the most important potion in the entire world. The W stands for Wherever. If you get to the magic great wall and pour the W-formula on top of it, a letter will come out. The letter K stands for the power behind the Legend of Karkatu. The rarest one is T for Teleportation."

Mr. Simon made sure they were listening and continued talking. "Today though, we will be talking about the Night of Magic Squares and the W-Formula in depth. And I am warning you, it is not easy. The Night of Magic Squares is a technique for defending not only yourselves, but the moon. These special squares are up in the pyramids and together create a golden sculpture. Everyone who has teleported to the Night of Magic Squares has tried to carry it with them and been blown away by the wind in seconds. Whoever can retrieve the Night of Magic Squares will stand out in history.

"Now, only if someone has the W-formula power from the magic great wall will they have a chance to even get up that pyramid. That piece of gold - it is so special." The students all looked fascinated.

"Okay, work time! Grab a pencil and paper. Now look at page 359. You will have to solve one important puzzle. You will read that the Night of Magic Squares is the second magical artifact that wizards and witches have come across. Please read the problem carefully and write down your answer. Not to brag, but nobody has solved this puzzle before. Except me, of course."

All three of them looked nervous.

Mr. Simon continued, "Okay, maybe I can give you a small hint. Once upon a time, I went snorkeling in the sea. There was a great magic orca swimming by my side, and I managed to befriend it!" Mr. Simon was obviously just saying gibberish and bragging about his skills, but while he crouched down and pretended that he was an orca, Matthew saw a sheet of paper on his desk. He couldn't see it clearly, but he noticed the paper reflected in the window to his right and noticed part of a word. It started with A-N-G. Matthew looked at the puzzle again and suddenly knew the answer to the Magic

Squares question: ANGORA 15. There were 9 squares that made up the Magic Square artifact. He knew from his math classes that the numbers 1 through 9 could be arranged in 3 rows and 3 columns to create a mathematical magic square that would add up to 15. You could add the numbers vertically, horizontally, or diagonally and always end up with a total of 15. This had to be part of the answer.

When their time was up, they stopped and gave Mr. Simon their sheets.

Mr. Simon took a minute to review their answers. "Unbelievable," he said, looking up at Matthew with great surprise. "You got it right."

He saw Victoria's jaw drop and Tom looked stunned. Matthew grinned as he walked out of the room.

* * *

Then they got to the Terrain Class and were greeted by Mr. Fire. This room was nothing like any other classroom they had been to. It had a big train set in the middle of the room which seemed to be on fire. But it wasn't hot, and the train set looked fine. Matthew eyed Mr. Fire closely and saw his Scuba Cube lying on the desk. But he did not ask anything about it yet.

"Hello!" said Mr. Fire. "I am your teacher for Terrain Class. Our curriculum is going to be about, believe it or not, Fire! Fi—" A loud ring cut him off.

Matthew saw that the ringing was coming from his Scuba Cube. He walked closer and saw that it was his mom and dad calling on FaceTime. "Press the red button!" he said to his teacher.

"Wait, I should flip the phone upside down?" asked Mr. Fire who was fascinated with the device.

Matthew grunted with frustration. "When you—" But before he could finish, Mr. Fire had pressed the accept button. Mr. Daniel was right there, and he started taking screenshots of Mr. Fire.

"Whoa!" yelled Mr. Fire. He was startled and threw the Scuba Cube up in the air. It kept on flipping so at one point Mr. Daniel had a perfect bird's eye view of the classroom. And in that split second, he took a screenshot.

Matthew heard his dad say, "Hello?" and then there was silence. Mr. Fire caught the phone and Matthew snatched it away from him. He would call his parents later when things were quiet.

"Let us carry on class!" said Mr. Fire.

The rest of the class was uneventful (besides Matthew almost burning Mr. Fire with the flick of his wand). They went on with the rest of their day.

Meanwhile, Mr. and Mrs. Daniel had invited back the inventor and tech person, Brown.

"So?" he asked. "How much information did you get?"

Mr. Daniel showed him the photo of when he had a perfect view of Mr. Fire's classroom.

"On the whiteboard it says Mr. Fire," said Mrs. Daniel. "I assume that this means Mr. Fire is a teacher and we are looking at his classroom."

Brown nodded. "Let us think this through step by step. First, send me everything you have. I need the photos and videos." Mr.

Daniel did as he was told. "Now I need to see your TV, okay? And in my bag, I have the rest of the equipment that we will need."

Mr. Daniel brought Brown to the room with a TV, and they sat down. "Let's hope this works," he said. He took out a cable and connected it to their TV. Then he went onto his phone. "I am connecting 'The Brown Cable' – which is a special cable I invented - to your TV, then I am going to use another cable after that. 'The Brown Cable Part 2' which will hopefully show us what is happening in that room right now. Finally, we will have to use 'The Brown Cable Part 3' which will show us a keypad. When we see that no one is in the room, we type in the code based on the coordinates of their location. All clear?" he asked and saw Mr. and Mrs. Daniel nodding.

"So, then we can move our mouse and make it touch the room there. We will have to wear these bracelets when we do that!" Brown exclaimed. He gave them silver bracelets. "Wear these. They will help us get to the room on the screen safely."

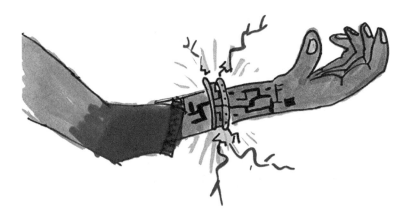

Mr. and Mrs. Daniel looked nervous but also excited. Brown tested all the connections and stood up. "Actually, let's plan our arrival in two days from now when the bracelets are strongest. They need more time to power up. We'll have a safer and stronger connection to get to Magic World."

Mr. Daniel looked disappointed. "Are you sure we can't try right now? I'm really worried about Matthew."

"I know it's not what you want to hear, but I'm sorry, we have to wait a little longer. We don't want to get lost between worlds with a weak connection," said Brown.

Mr. and Mrs. Daniel nodded. Getting lost on their way to Magic World did not sound appealing.

Back in Angora

Ms. Teach went up to Mr. Simon who was reading a book in his room. "What are you doing here?" he asked, not happy about the interruption.

"Simon! Can I have your G-Formula?" asked Ms. Teach sweetly.

Mr. Simon laughed. "My G-Formula will always be close to me! I would never part with it."

Ms. Teach suddenly looked serious. "I need it now. It's for an important cause."

"No! Why should I trust you? You know the formula can be dangerous in the wrong hands. I will never let you touch my G-Formula," said Mr. Simon, surprised at her request.

They looked at each other. "Orangu!" yelled Ms. Teach. The G-Formula flew out of Mr. Simon's desk. Ms. Teach was carefully trying to make the bottle float, but Mr. Simon jumped and knocked down the glass bottle.

"Gora G-Formula!" said Ms. Teach, just as the bottle was about to touch the ground. Then she pointed her wand at the bottle. A rock sprouted up with a cushion on it and the bottle fell on the cushion. Ms. Teach ran and put her hands on the formula, but Mr. Simon yelled, "Extravana Handcuff!" and flicked his wand.

Ms. Teach was handcuffed. But she smiled. "Looks like the Principal has taught you well," she said calmly. She did not look scared at all, quite the opposite in fact. "But has he taught you how to deflect these spells?" She froze for a second before saying, "Gola. Fiha!" The handcuffs flew onto Mr. Simon's hands. He struggled but could not get free. Ms. Teach poured a potion on Simon and he coughed.

"Now, I know that if anyone comes into the room, they will immediately see you. If I just trap you here and leave, I may be a suspect." Ms. Teach looked at him. "Seems like I am running out of ideas. But if I shift the focus away from me...." She smiled. "I'll be right back."

Ms. Teach teleported herself into Ms. Hopkins' room. Ms. Hopkins looked surprised to see her but before she could react, Ms. Teach cast a spell that put her into a deep sleep. She also made sure Ms. Hopkins would lose memory of the last hour. Ms. Teach laughed when she saw Ms. Hopkins had her necklace on.

"Oh, Hopkins! What a beautiful necklace you have," whispered Ms. Teach in a mocking voice. "Too bad it's going to be stolen!" She reached over and removed the necklace. It wouldn't come off. "Oh, that's right. Only you can remove it. Well, that's easy." She made sure Ms. Hopkins will still asleep and grabbed her hand to remove her own necklace. It worked.

Matthew, Victoria, and Tom were on their way to the Science Mag class later in the day, when they heard an announcement through the hallway speakers. "All teachers, report immediately to the teachers' lounge. Also, all classes are cancelled for the rest of the day. We repeat - no classes, and all teachers report to the lounge immediately!"

The teachers' lounge was soon packed with teachers curious about the sudden meeting with the Principal. "How many of us are gathered here?" asked Principal Terry.

The teachers counted. They ended the list with, "Ms.

Hopkins, Ms. Teach, Ms. Dorkey, Mr. Fire and Ms. Angela."

"Exactly!" yelled the Principal. "Ms. Ivan is missing. And Mr. Simon is not here. We cannot find them."

All the teachers gasped in astonishment.

"I have the security guards searching Ms. Ivan's room! And—"

A voice was heard through the intercom in the Principal's office. It was the head guard. "We found Mr. Simon! The handcuff spell is attached to him so he cannot talk, walk, or write. But we think we know who did this. It's Ms. Hopkins! We see her necklace right next to him on the ground. She must have dropped it. And we think he is nodding his head that it's her."

One of the teachers started crying and the rest looked very worried. "After a few months of Ms. Angela's healing he will be back to normal. I promise," said the Principal. He looked extremely concerned.

"Do you have any word on Ms. Ivan?" he asked, but sadly the head guard did not. "Keep up the good work! We have Hopkins here and will speak to her. She will know where Ms. Ivan is."

Ms. Hopkins was speechless. She looked down at her neck. The light wasn't reflecting off her necklace as it did before. It was bare.

"But it is not me!" she yelled. Ms. Teach snorted at this.

Ms. Hopkins twitched her eyes at her . "It is you!" she said. "I don't why I didn't say anything earlier about your evil ideas." She grew desperate trying to prove her innocence. "No! How can it be me? I was teaching when Ms. Ivan went missing. I'm sure it is Ms. Teach. Haven't you seen her going behind our backs trying to convince teachers to do strange things?"

"Enough!" shouted the Principal. "We know who the villain is. We have proof that it's you, Ms. Hopkins. No one can remove your necklace except you. Clearly you were foolish enough to drop it. Now please leave before I completely lose my temper. You are to no longer remain at this school."

Ms. Hopkins slowly walked out of the room with her head down. "This isn't fair," she whispered softly.

Up in his room, Matthew had a view of magic police cars dancing across the road. He looked confused. "Um... Victoria, have you ever seen a crime being committed in this school?"

Victoria looked puzzled. "No."

Matthew took a breath. "Then why are there police cars here?"

"What?" yelled Victoria. "Wait, we have a clear view through the window!" They saw Ms. Hopkins being escorted out of the school.

"She did not commit a crime," said Victoria, who was very upset. "I've had a post-it note tracking Ms. Teach. It is usually super dependable. It will follow the person whose name you write on it and report back where they are and what they're doing. It will all be listed on the post-it note. But the note I sent could not find Ms. Teach. She must have used a spell to throw off anyone or anything following her. She's the one who should be arrested, not Ms. Hopkins!"

Matthew looked shaken. "Ms. Hopkins has always been very respectful and nice. But maybe she did something bad while she was in Non-Magic World."

Tom shook his head. "There were magic security cameras watching her, remember? I don't think she's done anything wrong. And now the cameras here aren't working...Something seems fishy."

Matthew and Victoria spoke at the same time. "We need to help Ms. Hopkins."

"I am going out to get some answers. Stay right here," said Victoria as she ran out of the room.

It was a half hour before Victoria came back to them. "I got some information from Ms. Angela. Actually, I got a lot of information. When the emergency meeting was called, the teachers went to the Principal's office. But Mr. Simon and, of course, Ms. Ivan were missing. Soon they got word from Principal Terry's guards. They found Mr. Simon in his room in the big handcuff spell! He will need about six months to heal. But that is too long to wait to find out the truth. The school guards saw Mr. Simon in handcuffs and saw Ms. Hopkins' necklace right next to it. That's why everyone thinks it must be her. She always has her necklace on."

But Tom was quick to defend Ms. Hopkins. "It can't be her. I have a concrete reason too." He explained. "When we were in Mr. Simon's class and went to get Matthew's books, we heard Ms. Hopkins snoring in the other room. Also, her alarm was set to 10 a.m. and Ms. Hopkins never gets up before her alarm rings unless there is an emergency call. Which there was when Principal Terry made the announcement. And we know that Mr. Simon's handcuffing happened before the emergency meeting ended. It's not Ms. Hopkins!"

Victoria nodded. "I agree with you. Ms. Hopkins seems like an honest person. I do think she's mixed up in something odd though. I don't trust that Ms. Hopkins happened to lose her necklace in Mr. Simon's room. We need to investigate this. I think we're almost certain Ms. Teach is doing bad stuff but first we need to find some evidence. Then we have to find out if she is working for someone or if someone else is working for her."

Matthew nodded while Tom quietly said, "Let's do this."

CHAPTER SIX

IN WITH THE GIANT

Sometime last year

The bullies started walking towards their target who was a younger kid in school. These bad little Jokers held out their fists, but Terry stopped them.

"No punching allowed," said Ms. Teach, who was behind Terry. "Terry, as Boo Boo Magic teacher I think I know the best way to teach them a lesson."

Terry nodded. "Okay Ms. Teach, please, these are our students after all, and we must teach them what is right and what is wrong. I do not want anyone in Angora to get hurt."

"Neither do I Terry, neither do I," remarked Ms. Teach. She smiled as she dragged the bullies outside Angora's walls. Then she started kicking them.

"You almost blew our cover with your behavior – and you have made a bad impression in front of the Principal." The bullies were groaning and holding on to their stomachs. "Luckily, Terry's power has weakened over the years," continued Ms. Teach, "so we are closer to reaching our goal. Angora will fall. He will rise out of the darkness, and you will be the ones to make sure our path to victory is clear..."

Present day

Matthew looked puzzled. "How can we prove Ms. Hopkins is innocent?" he asked.

"How can we do it?" Victoria responded with a question and looked at them. "Ok, we are sure it was not Ms. Hopkins. We suspect Ms. Teach. There is one person that obviously knows who it is and can give Terry answers - Mr. Simon."

Matthew did not understand this. "He is literally handcuffed and can no longer speak or move. And you told us it will take a long time for even a magic nurse to heal him. Do you really think we have the power to get those handcuffs off him?" He thought he was asking a ridiculous question.

"Besides," said Tom, "we don't even know for sure where Mr. Simon is right now. The next Night of Magic Squares class is only tomorrow. Rumor is he spends time in his class to heal, but how do we confirm that?"

Victoria nodded. "I understand the challenges. But we'll have to give it a try," she said. "I have an idea."

Outside Angora, Ms. Hopkins was walking in the woods, trying to sort out the mess she was in. The magic police had forbidden her from going too far from Angora until the investigation was over. She was trying to figure out how her necklace was removed without her knowledge and permission.

To her surprise, Ms. Teach showed up. "Hello, Hopkins.

Now you see me for who I really am, don't you? I'm sure you know my true identity by now."

Ms. Hopkins turned red with embarrassment. "I should have realized earlier. Way earlier. I just didn't recognize you until recently. You look so – different."

Ms. Teach nodded. "Well, since you have finally figured out who I am, I'd say a fight is called for. Sister against sister."

"You are right, Ms. Teach. My sister...It's a shame it has to be this way. We were once so close," remarked Ms. Hopkins. "But you've gotten me out of Angora. Why not just leave me alone?"

Ms. Teach raised her wand. "I can't trust you. I gave you so many chances to join me. And now I have my orders. Too bad your magic has weakened without your necklace. Dramatica despell!"

Ms. Hopkins tried to move out of the way, but she wasn't fast enough. Daggers started coming straight at her. At the last second, she jumped, and the daggers slammed into the ground. Ms. Teach raised her wand once more. "Isara."

Lava started to pour out from a bottle that appeared suddenly, and it almost hit Ms. Hopkins. This time, she jumped into a small bush.

"Why bother hiding?" snarled Ms. Teach. "You can't get

away."

Ms. Hopkins suddenly sprinted out of a bush on the other side of Ms. Teach and tackled her, grabbing her wand.

"Nowhere to go now," said Ms. Hopkins out of breath. Ms. Teach grunted but managed to pull something out of her pocket. It was a red wand. "Forgot I like to carry an extra wand, didn't you?"

She stretched her hand and pointed her wand at Ms. Hopkins. "Shanqai," she yelled but before the spell could hit her, Ms. Hopkins leaned back, and the spell hit the grass. Ms. Teach stood up, looking frustrated. "I am wasting my time here. All these spells will draw the attention of the police. I'll handle you later," she said abruptly. She started to teleport back to school. But Ms. Hopkins tackled her to the ground mid-teleportation.

"Terry taught you that move, didn't he, Lisa," Ms. Teach said. They were both on the ground but the wand in Ms. Hopkin's hand had leapt into Ms. Teach's hand. "You're weak and vulnerable and can't help Angora. So why bother with you." And just like that, Ms. Teach actually did teleport away.

Back in school, Victoria and Tom were debating their options intently. "It has to be done," she said. "I know that you are going to say no, but either Ms. Hopkins is gone and a teacher who is evil gets away with it, or this has to happen."

She looked pleadingly at Matthew and Tom. Matthew guessed that he was expected to be the decision maker in this situation.

"Fine!" he yelled feeling pressured. "Do it, Victoria."

Victoria smiled. "Sorry Tom, but we need to try this whether you like it or not." She walked into Ms. Angela's office to ask for permission to visit Mr. Simon. "It is definitely for learning purposes," she said again. "I want to observe Mr. Simon to document the symptoms of the handcuff spell."

Ms. Angela was not a gullible person, but she also knew that Victoria liked studying. "Fine, I will allow this to happen, but I must consult with Terry first."

Victoria shook her head. "No, please let me go right away. Everyone is so upset with what's happened. I don't want to bother the Principal with this request right now. And anyway, you must be tired after what you have faced today, right, Ms. Angela? So please just let me go. I'll only be there for five minutes and will write down everything I see and try to cheer up Mr. Simon."

Ms. Angela exhaled slowly. "Fine, I guess. You'll find him in his classroom. The nurse thought he would heal faster in a familiar environment."

Victoria thanked her as she started running back to the group E room. When she got there, she saw Tom curled up in a ball in the room.

"Please say that she said no," said Tom. Victoria smiled. "She said yes, I can visit him."

Tom sighed. "Why does the world have to be so confusing?" They started to walk out of their classroom towards Mr. Simon.

They were spotted by the bullies, led by Alexander. His blue eyes flashed with anger. "Ms. Teach gave us orders and we follow them. The cameras are still off so as long as we don't get caught, we are fine. It is time for Matthew to be facing a whole lot of darkness."

One of the other students in the group smirked. "This is even easier than I expected. They're walking right towards us. Come on, we'll capture them now and then teleport out of school."

A girl named Ava took out her wand and whispered, "Mminas." Water gushed out of the lockers in the hallway and splashed at Matthew and the others.

Tom glanced at where the water was coming from and shivered. He saw the bullies ahead of them, watching and waiting. "Let's get out of here," he said, and they ran back to their group E room, slamming the door shut and locking it.

"It's the bullies. Don't they know you can't use spells against other students in this school?" Matthew started to panic as he heard splashes coming from all around.

"We'll get you Matthew," someone screamed and unfortunately no one was around to help the group E kids. "Why do they want me?" asked Matthew. "I'm new here and I don't even know a single spell."

Victoria shrugged. "I have no idea. But they mean business. We need to escape." Matthew looked thoughtful. "If we huddle up here, they'll get us. Maybe we should talk to them."

Tom shook his head. "Nobody can talk reason with the

bullies. When they find their target and aim for it, they are unstoppable, and it seems like you are their target, Matthew."

"They're evil," said Matthew. "I don't think they are doing this on their own though. Someone must be ordering them around."

"You think everyone who doesn't like you is evil," said Victoria rolling her eyes. "But this time, I believe you."

Matthew clapped his hands. "I have a plan. If all they want is me, I can lure them away from here and take them somewhere they won't want to be seen doing anything messy. We still want to help Ms. Hopkins, so Victoria, I'd say that you go to Mr. Simon. Tom, it would be great if someone could stand guard in group E in case anything happens here."

Tom nodded happily. "Be careful," he said.

"So, I guess we have a plan." Matthew unlocked the door quickly and stepped out. The bullies were right outside, waiting as he expected. He might not be as tough as the bullies, but he was faster than them, and started to run full speed down the hall. The bullies came right after him. This left a clearing for Victoria. She ran into Mr. Simon's room. Mr. Simon couldn't talk, of course, but he pulled his shoulders up as though asking what in the world Victoria was doing.

"I am here to save you. Let's get rid of those handcuffs," she said, and Mr. Simon widened his eyes in surprise.

Meanwhile, Matthew stared into the bullies' eyes and all he could see was anger. They all held out their wands and Matthew started running, trying to avoid their shots. He hoped to find a grown-up he could trust. One of the bullies shouted out a spell and it hit Matthew in the leg. He stumbled and fell down a flight of stairs. The bullies did not want to get caught so they decided to quietly carry Matthew up the stairs to the group J room on the highest floor. Matthew tried kicking and screaming, but they punched him to keep him quiet. They threw him into the room. Matthew had never been in this room before. There was brown icky mud everywhere and the beds had vines growing all over.

"It must suck living in this group," he thought.

Alexander got out his wand. "You are never going to get away with this," Matthew said to Alexander as he got kicked onto the vines. This place was the opposite of luxury.

"Capture or kill?" asked one of the bullies. Alexander gave Matthew an evil grin and raised his hand. "Capture."

The bullies got out a little syringe. "So, Matthew, ever gotten a magic shot? They don't hurt, but they itch." Alexander ferociously stuck the needle into Matthew's arm and pulled it out. Matthew could see his blood collected in a vial. "Perfect. Now we hide him somewhere."

The group got up and started looking around the room. Alexander said, "We make him invisible and find a corner somewhere to hide him." The others nodded. Alexander and the bullies looked away for a few seconds to find a good hiding spot. All they really saw was vines and mud though. "The vines can be a good hiding spot," said one of the bullies, but when they turned around, they saw that Matthew was not there.

"What? Get him," Alexander said, as he saw Matthew quietly opening the door.

"Quickly, he cannot get away. Attack him!" The bullies raised their wands and ran out of the room to see Matthew zipping down the stairs. He suddenly stopped and started scratching his arm where he had received the shot a few minutes ago. The bullies took advantage and started firing arrows at Matthew. Matthew looked up in time and dodged the arrows. He jumped and landed at the bottom of the stairs. "No! Don't let him escape!" Matthew could hear Alexander screaming as he ran away at top speed.

Back in the group E room, Tom was sitting at a desk eating a cookie when he heard a little creak, and someone coughed. "Who's there?" he asked immediately, raising his wand.

"Don't worry, Tom, it's just me." Ms. Hopkins appeared, stepping out through a vent in the room. She was covered in mud and had blood along her eyebrow from the fight with Ms. Teach.

"What?" said Tom. He looked at her seriously. "How did you get in here?"

"I am here because I snuck in. Well, I wasn't exactly successful in sneaking in because one of the guards saw me, but anyway."

Tom was speechless. "You crawled through a pipe and then the vent?"

Ms. Hopkins nodded. "Where are Matthew and Victoria?"

Tom shrugged. "Matthew is being chased by the bullies who are being crazy right now. Victoria is trying to get Mr. Simon to speak so that he can say that you are innocent. Oh yeah, I know you are innocent, and we are going to find out who did it."

Ms. Hopkins teared up as she looked at Tom. "I appreciate that. I know who it did," she said quietly. "It's Ms. Teach. I should have called her out a long time ago, but we just got into a little fight and also she's my sis— never mind." She paused. "So, you are right now clueless about what's happening outside this room?"

Tom nodded. "Clueless seems to be the right word."

Matthew was still running and running. The bullies were aiming more arrows at him, but none of them seemed to be getting close. Matthew thought that he was safe but did not notice Alexander right behind him, with a wand to his back. "Your life is over, Matthew, it really is. I am not sparing you. Orienthu!"

A vine came out of nowhere, and instead of hitting Matthew's back, the spell deflected off the vine and hit the ceiling. Alexander saw a hole in the ceiling and gulped. Then, in front of him he saw Mr. Fire.

"Sorry, Alexander, but you have been caught attacking another student. I can't see any option but to expel you from Angora. We have a zero-tolerance policy for this type of behavior. Your parents will be alerted shortly. Prepare to leave the school...Now!"

Matthew took the opportunity to escape into the group E

room with Ms. Hopkins and Tom. After he realized Ms. Hopkins was there, they hugged each other, and he shared the news that Alexander and the other bullies were going to be expelled.

"I got lucky," he said, "It was scary up there in Group J's room. They gave me a shot for some reason, some magic shot."

Ms. Hopkins smacked her lips. "They wanted to draw your blood. They tease people all the time, but they were trying something more serious with you. We must look into this more carefully when we have the chance. But for now, it is fine. At least we have the bullies out of Angora territory. And I really hope Victoria has good luck removing the handcuffs.

"Now, Matthew, I have a job for you. There is a guard that spotted me when I was getting into the pipes, and he is going to report that to the Principal any minute. Distract the Principal until Victoria proves my innocence. Terry might force me out of Magic World for good if the guard tells him what he saw, and they catch me. The guard that spotted me has a sailor's hat. Make sure he doesn't talk to the Principal before I am proved innocent." Matthew nodded as he went out of the room.

Ms. Hopkins waited until Matthew was down the hall before turning to Tom. "Tom, it does not have to be a secret. I'll make sure they don't blackmail you," she said but Tom shook his head.

"Not even my mom knows my secret, why would I tell anyone here. They'll think that I'm cursed. You know Hornet – he'll try to get me on his side."

Ms. Hopkins sighed. "Tom, the more you hold back, the more difficult it will be for people to help you when the time comes." Tom gulped. "Ms. Hopkins, let's not talk about this right now."

Squeezing his hands together he raised his voice begging for Ms. Hopkins to listen. "It is a part of my identity that is private. No one can know. I trust you, Ms. Hopkins, make sure nobody finds out!"

* * *

Back in Mr. Simon's office, Victoria was examining his handcuffs from every single angle. "No, I can't take it off like that, then your mouth would be crooked. I can't put on the bee sting spell, no... Wait! I know what to do." She got out her wand and started to think. She thought back to the book Matthew had stolen from Mr. Simon's office. She remembered a profile on a magician who taught at Angora briefly. He was a whiz at reversing spells like this, but it was considered dangerous. Victoria wasn't sure how much of a risk she could take trying out a spell based on what she remembered. But what was the other option...

Meanwhile, Matthew wondered how to find the security guard with the sailor hat. He wondered why Ms. Hopkins hadn't requested Tom to do it. "Why did she make me help her?" Matthew wondered. There had to be a reason. Even if the guard tells the Principal that Ms. Hopkins snuck into Angora and she is banished from the school once more, what's the big deal? Once Victoria proves Ms. Hopkins' innocence, she would anyway be okay. Matthew felt like he was being bossed around in this situation. "Ms. Hopkins wanted me out of the room, but why?" He decided to put this question on hold.

Suddenly, Matthew spotted the guard. He did not have time to thoroughly examine the hat, since he was running, but he was quite sure this was the right person. Matthew started chasing after him. He knew that he was faster than the guard, but he would never be able to find out where the Principal's office was unless he followed him. Just as they entered a hallway that had a sign pointing to the Principal's office, he yelled out, "Security guard! Sir, there's an emergency and we need your help!"

The guard turned around surprised. "What is it? What happened?"

Matthew had to think fast. "Um...It's an explosion! In the science lab near Group F's room. I hope no one's hurt." He tried to sound as convincing as possible.

The guard looked shocked. "Let's go right away."

"You go ahead," said Matthew. "I need to inform Principal Terry and we'll join you with more help. Please go, this is urgent."

The guard nodded and ran in the opposite direction. Matthew walked into Terry's office.

"Principal Terry - it's an emergency – come with me right now!" said Matthew.

"Matthew! What is it? What's wrong?" asked Terry concerned. He gave Principal Terry the same story about an explosion but this time he said it was near Group G's room.

The Principal gasped. "Oh, no! Let's go. Does the security team know?" Matthew nodded. "They're on their way." He lied. He closed his eyes for two seconds. He knew he was getting himself into tons of trouble with these lies. Terry and Matthew started running towards Group G's class. Matthew still had a burning question that he wanted to ask Principal Terry, and now was the perfect time.

"What?" asked Terry, knowing that something was troubling Matthew. Matthew took a deep breath in and out. He couldn't describe what he was feeling. Frustration? Confusion? He spit it out.

"What is so special about your wand?" he asked. His eyes started to burn into Terry's hand which was clutching his wand. "Black ninjas? It seems a bit childish for a very powerful wizard!"

Terry smacked his lips. "I heard you requested the same wand. I'm sorry you didn't get it. This wand is special because it is the Wand of Slavery! I want to tell you about it, but it will have to wait for another time. Right now let's get this crisis under control."

Back in Mr. Simon's room, Victoria closed her eyes and prayed for the courage and skill to do this spell right. And then in a blink of an eye Victoria freed Mr. Simon. But it was more complicated than she expected. Mr. Simon started coughing and stood up, then ended up falling on the ground. He had his hands on his head, felt dizzy, and when he saw Victoria, he suddenly twitched his eyebrows up into a nervous glance.

"It's your friend!" he yelled. "He did it. Matthew - I hate

80

that boy."

Victoria looked shocked. "What?" she whispered. "Did you mean to say Ms. Teach did it? It can't be Matthew. That's impossible – he was with me around the time you were put into handcuffs."

Mr. Simon looked confused for a second but Ms. Teach's grip on his mind was still strong. The only thought that kept coming to him was Matthew stealing his book. He must be responsible for his condition as well. Mr. Simon was still weak but crawled to the wall and pulled the emergency alarm. Sirens started to blare through the school. A minute later, Principal Terry and Matthew ran into the room. They looked surprised to see Mr. Simon on the ground without his handcuffs.

Mr. Simon pointed at Matthew. "It's the new boy! He handcuffed me!"

Terry hesitated and watched Mr. Simon closely. "Are you sure? Matthew is new here – and so young – how could he have performed such a complicated spell?"

More and more security guards and teachers started running into the room to see what was happening. Someone managed to switch off the alarm so now there was silence. Mr. Simon said again, this time with more confidence. "It was Matthew."

There was stunned silence in the room. Then everyone started talking at once. Terry stood up on a chair and clapped his hands. He yelled loudly, "Enough! Everybody out. The only ones to stay behind are Matthew, Victoria, and Mr. Simon. I need to speak to them in private."

The others started grumbling and showed their disapproval, but they agreed and left the room. Terry pointed to those in the room. "Sit," he said sternly. "I don't know what is going on here, but I want the truth." Everyone sat around a table. "Victoria, how in Magic World did you manage to free Mr. Simon from the spell? The rest of us, including the best healers here, thought it would take months for him to heal."

Victoria shrugged. "Honestly, I can't fully explain it myself. But the answers were all written in a book that we came across recently. A teacher once—"

Mr. Simon cut her off. "Thank you for the details, Victoria, but you forgot to mention that this was the book you stole - or Matthew stole - from my library. I have trackers on all my books, by the way. You all took it even though you knew it was against the principles of Angora. And you thought you were smart to have Matthew put the spell on me and then Victoria pretends to find the cure in the book to free me. Do you really deny this?"

Victoria shook her head. "Please listen - the first part about taking the book is true, but we would never put a spell on you. We really wanted to figure out a way to free you. And part of the reason was so you could save Ms. Hopkins from being accused of something she didn't do."

Matthew spoke up. "Principal Terry, please trust me, I have to show you something important." The Principal raised an eyebrow. "Like that explosion you told me about?"

Matthew gave a weak smile. "As you guessed, that was fake but for a good reason. And I'll show you what that reason is. Follow me – please."

Terry sighed and started to walk out of the room after Matthew. Victoria and Mr. Simon quietly followed them. They went into the Group E room and saw Tom and Ms. Hopkins. Ms. Hopkins got up, not sure how everyone was going to react. Victoria ran towards her and hugged her.

"What are you doing here?" Terry asked, shocked. "How did you manage to get in?"

"We'll explain later," jumped in Matthew. "Right now, I'm worried about what Mr. Simon is saying about me. I want Ms. Hopkins to hear it too." Ms. Hopkins listened quietly as Victoria quickly explained how she had managed to reverse the handcuff spell. She then told her that Mr. Simon immediately reacted by accusing Matthew of attacking him and putting him under a spell.

Ms. Hopkins shook her head. "Wow, the handcuff spell might be reversed now but Ms. Teach probably put a formula on Simon to erase his memory of what happened. He's pulling from his last memory that was saved, which was probably Matthew taking the book."

Terry looked more confused than ever. "Are you saying Ms. Teach is behind this? I don't know who to believe." Simon started to look less confident and more miserable now. Were his memories of what happened really blocked?

Terry made a decision. "We're not going to resolve this now. There are too many accusations flying around and I need more time to investigate. I can't take the word of some students and Ms. Hopkins who was just dismissed from the school recently. Think of how the teachers, students and all the parents will react? This could become a major scandal. I suggest no one leaves Angora for the next few days until we figure this out. And I need to speak to Ms. Teach right away."

Ms. Hopkins looked relieved. "I think that's the right strategy, Terry." Simon continued to look upset. But he finally acknowledged that Victoria had saved him.

"Thank you, Victoria," he said quietly. "I'm going to go to my room to rest now." As he was leaving, Mr. Simon gave Matthew an evil look. Matthew was tempted to stick his tongue out at him but stopped himself. He had to try to be mature and responsible while they figured out the truth.

Matthew, Victoria, and Tom walked up to their room together. "So much drama," said Tom, shaking his head. He saw the now famous book sitting on the table in their room. "This seems to be a powerful book. Let me examine it." He opened it to the first page and stared at the Table of Contents.

Angora Teachers

1. Simon
2. Hopkins
3. Ivan
4. Fire

5. Angela
6. Teach
7. Fire the Second
8. Terry
9. Hornet

"Fire the Second?" said Tom looking up from the book. "And Hornet? Who are they?" he asked even though he knew who Hornet was.

Even Victoria looked surprised for a change. "Never heard of them," she said. She flipped to the chapter on Hornet.

Hornet: Cause of the War of Quarthon!

It was blank. "That's strange," said Victoria. Matthew examined the page. "It doesn't look like anything is printed in invisible ink. Why is this chapter blank? This Hornet is unlucky to have no information written about him."

"I kind of know what the war of Quarthon is. I am pretty sure it was a war a long time ago and Angora was in the middle of it. The villains wanted Angora, but I have no idea how Hornet is connected to this history," Tom said.

Victoria shrugged. "Doesn't matter, we have more serious problems right now."

* * *

In Non-Magic World, Mr. Daniel, Mrs. Daniel, and Brown stared at the clock. "It's time," said Mrs. Daniel both excited and a little scared. The three of them wore their bracelets. A portal popped up a few seconds later. "We're going in there!" said

Brown as he led the way.

* * *

Matthew woke up with a start. He had fallen asleep with a lot on his mind. He could hear a little bird pecking on his window. Matthew was no longer sleepy and wanted to wake up Victoria and Tom to talk to them. But just then he heard a beeping noise. He got out of bed and followed the sound. Soon he was outside Mr. Fire's classroom. Matthew knocked on the door to see if Mr. Fire was in there.

"Mr. Fire – are you okay? What's that beeping sound?"

The door opened except Mr. Fire wasn't there. Standing face to face with Matthew was Mrs. Daniel. He froze, unable to believe his eyes. "Mom! You're here! How is this possible?"

Mrs. Daniel squealed and hugged him. "I'm so happy we could make it."

Matthew was grinning from ear to ear. "How did you find me?" Just then he noticed someone standing behind his mom. It was the best hacker he knew. "Brown? *The* Brown?"

Brown smiled hearing his name. "I can proudly say that's me!"

When Matthew saw Mr. Daniel, he ran and gave him a big hug. "I can't believe you're here. I'm sure you were worried about me. Did you give Adam and everyone else an explanation for why I'm not there?"

Mr. Daniel replied, "Yes, I gave your school a call and said you won a scholarship and had to leave right away for a year

86

traveling and studying on a ship. I'm not sure they believed me. Everyone is talking about how you and Ms. Hopkins showed up at the bank and all this crazy stuff about smoke and magic. Goliath is suspicious. And she says she misses torturing you in class."

Mrs. Daniel nudged Mr. Daniel. "Come on, let's tell him the news."

Mr. Daniel nodded. "Um... Brown, please give us some privacy. We have something to tell Matthew." Mr. and Mrs. Daniel looked really happy. "We are thrilled to be with you. And we wanted to share the news that we are going to have a baby. You will be a big brother!"

Matthew was stunned. "Wow! Really?" He hugged his parents again, still amazed that they were with him in Angora.

The residents in Angora, in the meantime, all started to hear a beeping sound too in their rooms. The appearance of non-magical visitors had triggered an alarm. Soon, many people started walking into Mr. Fire's classroom to see who was there. Mrs. Daniel looked nervous, but Mr. Daniel stood confidently by the door and introduced himself to the first person who walked in - Terry. "Hello, I hope you don't mind us showing up unexpectedly in the middle of the night. We are Matthew's parents. It's nice to meet you."

"I recognized you from pictures on Matthew's Scuba Cube," said Terry. They were all standing together in Mr. Fire's room. Terry smiled at them happily but didn't admit that he was scared on the inside. "Hello, visitors. No one non-magical has ever made it to Magic World, so um... Congratulations, I guess."

Mr. and Mrs. Daniel smiled, and Brown was super enthusiastic. "Do you have any precious jewels here? Any gold?" As soon as he asked the question Mr. Daniel squeezed Brown's hand to stop him from saying more.

"He meant to say that it is not cold here. Your school is so cozy and welcoming," clarified Mr. Daniel.

Terry sighed with relief now, nodding. Then the security team barged down the stairs. "Terry, we came down here as soon as we heard the news. Are you okay?" He smiled politely. "Don't worry, I am just fine."

The security team looked at the three strange visitors in the eyes. "They are not robots," one said almost immediately, but it took some time for the rest to make sure. They checked their body with a stick. "Good - they come with no weapons."

All the teachers started barging down the stairs now. Ms. Teach was the first one to comment. "Intruders!" she hollered.

Terry raised his eyebrows. "They are not intruders, and anyway – as we discussed earlier today at our meeting - you do not have the right to make any accusations. Stand back."

Ms. Teach glowered at all the teachers. "Do you think that we should be friends with non-magical people? Remember what we've talked about," she said glaring at them. Clearly, she had been having conversations with many of them about her plans. The teachers glanced at Terry nervously as though waiting for him to say something.

"Are you really just going to wait for him to talk? No!" Ms. Teach stomped her feet. "Just help me destroy these intruders already."

Mrs. Daniel gave a little scream. Terry looked at the group carefully. "Hold on, let's—"

But most of the teachers weren't listening and started moving towards Ms. Teach to show that they were on her side. Even some of the security guards joined her. "Yes!" said Ms. Teach. "See? You have to give them a chance to make their own decisions."

Terry glanced at her in anger. "You are controlling them now, just like you did with Mr. Simon, isn't it? Must be proud of yourself for performing that handcuff spell."

Ms. Teach chuckled. "You finally guessed, but too late, now they are all switching to my side." Terry looked like he had just seen a ghost, but this was a million times worse. Suddenly, the least expected thing happened.

Ms. Hopkins appeared out of nowhere and stood next to Terry. She clapped her hands, but everyone ignored her. Ms. Teach and her followers pointed their wands at the three visitors.

"Everybody!" said Ms. Hopkins in her loudest voice. "Please listen. Look at what you are doing. You are doing the opposite of what Angora is supposed to stand for. We are supposed to welcome new visitors, but you are looking to destroy them. These are Matthew's parents. And his friend," she said looking at Brown. "Opposing them when we know nothing about them is not right. They are probably scared of us and just want to be with their son."

Ms. Hopkins managed to knock some sense into the teachers, and they looked embarrassed and sympathetic as they saw Mrs. Daniel hugging the wall as though she could walk through it for extra safety.

Now there was a long line of people facing Ms. Teach, and they did not look pleased. Terry spoke up. "Ms. Teach, sorry, but your plan has backfired. Plus, you have confessed in front of everyone about your attack on Mr. Simon." Mr. Simon grunted when he heard his name. He still looked puzzled, clearly not yet fully recovered from the spell.

Ms. Teach started to back away. Now she was hugging the wall like Mrs. Daniel, trying to get away. The security guards walked towards her to make an arrest.

Terry said, "Please hand over your wand. We don't want to fight." But Ms. Teach was one step ahead and held her wand out in front of her. Boom! In a flash, she was gone. She had teleported out of Angora.

* * *

Matthew was sitting in the library. He had told his parents he needed to finish some homework, but the truth was, he wanted to be alone for a little while. He was excited by the news that he was going to be a big brother soon, but also scared. There were already so many changes in his life and he wasn't sure how a new sibling would fit in. But it felt selfish to have these thoughts. He didn't know what to do.

* * *

Meanwhile, Brown was invited to a meeting by Terry. All the teachers were assembled together. Terry cleared his throat. "We have an issue, Brown. Since you are an amazing inventor and programmer, and also an amazing hacker, we want you to work on a project for us. In return, we can give you an um... a good amount of gold!"

Brown smiled when he heard the word gold. Finally, something to get excited about.

"You cannot mess up on this project because it is too important. And, it involves a little bit of magic law breaking," said Terry. "We cannot tell you everything because, well, this is Magic World, but we can tell you some parts that you need to know."

"Then let us have some tea and cake and discuss!" said Brown who was getting hungry.

Terry looked confused. "Excuse me?" he asked. "Tea and cake should be served at a time of celebration. Now focus. You need to hack into Ms. Teach's computer system. I'll give you more information on her, but I want you to find out how she managed to turn off the magic security cameras. We need to get them working again. I also want you to track down where she is. Does that sound okay?" Brown nodded. "Good, let's get going."

"All the pieces are in play," said Angela who was in the room listening, but Ms. Dorkey shook her head. She didn't seem convinced that Brown was the solution to their problems with Ms.

Teach.

* * *

"Let's focus - I have no time to waste. None of this yip yap nonsense!" said Mr. Fire fiercely as he strolled along. Matthew settled into his Terrain Class and was starting to open his notebook when he heard Mr. Fire muttering to himself. "I can't believe what I am doing with my life! A Terrain teacher!"

Matthew, Victoria, and Tom glanced at each other. Didn't he know they could hear him? Victoria asked him in a serious tone, "Mr. Fire, is anything bothering you?"

Mr. Fire laughed quietly. "Not at all, my dear." His voice sounded different, and he looked stiff.

"Um... Can you give us a recap of what we learned in our last summer class?" asked Victoria.

Matthew looked at her surprised. She had an amazing memory. Why would Victoria of all people ask him for a recap?

"I think trainer cards?" said Mr. Fire, not making eye contact.

"What's that?" asked Victoria but Matthew knew that she knew what trainer cards were. "We didn't learn about them last time."

"Well, I thought that is what he taught you. I mean what I taught you. I mean, class dismissed!"

Mr. Fire looked agitated. Matthew thought he didn't look well. They quietly said their goodbyes and left the room.

* * *

"I have recovered one security camera for you," Brown told Terry. "I haven't figured everything out, but I'm able to bypass whatever spell was put on the system."

Terry nodded. "Well, there are a few more to go!"

"Also, I found some information," continued Brown. "On that crazy lady Ms. Teach."

The Principal raised an eyebrow. "What information?"

But Brown just held out his hand. "Money, please."

Terry sighed. "We'll give you an extra $100,000." Brown looked pleased with himself. He nodded satisfied.

* * *

Matthew was trying to find his parents now that he was done with classes. He started to walk to the group E room, expecting they were there, but then a voice rang out in Matthew's head, one he had never heard before. It sounded like gurgling water.

"You lost," said the voice in his head. "You will never succeed." The voice got fainter and fainter. Matthew started to walk fast, confused by these sounds. Ding! He felt a big wave of energy go down his body pushing him forwards. He walked up the steps unwillingly. "Bong! Dong! Ding!" Three more shocks moved down his body. The voice returned and said, "The ghost will be recreated in another form as the first one kills you! Ding!" He felt one more shock. Matthew was at the top of the stairs. "You have just seen the first of my plans! Ding!" Matthew was pulled into the group J room and hoped the sound in his head would stop. It surprisingly did.

But not before he heard one last word. "Trapped." Then the door shut behind him.

* * *

"He's gone!" said Mr. Daniel as Mrs. Daniel started to sob. "We've been trying to find him all day and no one knows where he is. He called us this morning saying he wanted to see us after his morning class. He was last seen in class with Mr. Fire."

"We are checking the entire school," said Terry. "Unfortunately, our security system was switched off with some tricky magic and we are trying to get it fixed. But he is going to be here. Don't worry."

"I hope that evil woman hasn't taken him away," said Mrs. Daniel sniffling.

Suddenly a loud horn started to blow. Terry looked at his computer closely. "Three more security cameras have been tackled! Thank you," he said to no one in particular.

Brown walked into the room just then and gave an update. "I'm detecting her on my system. Ms. Teach is coming towards us with a cosmic force that will destroy this school, and according to my calculations, there is going to be a tornado. I don't know about all of you – but I'm getting out of here."

Terry looked at Brown's device. "That is no ordinary tornado that is coming!" he gulped. "That is a blackout. Based on its speed, we only have a day to get organized. We have to get all of our people to the front line and prepare for battle."

Mr. Daniel grumbled at Terry's comments. "What are you

saying? What is this blackout and what do you mean there is going to be a battle?"

Terry looked exhausted already. "I hate to tell you this, but you picked the worst time to visit. A blackout in Magic World means the sun might explode. And it looks like Ms. Teach is bringing an army with her to take over the school."

"No!" yelled Mr. Daniel. "My son is still in danger and now you're talking about a battle? What is this place! Stop talking about the blackout. We need to focus on finding my son right now!"

A few floors above in room J, Matthew was trying to find a way to escape. A piece of paper on the floor suddenly caught his eye. "The Heart of Magic," he read and at the bottom he saw the words Magic Wall.

Matthew read the article that followed.

The Magic Wall
Written by: Tori Nicholas

The Magic Wall is a border between your true self, and the self you want to be. The Magic Wall is either a physical wall, or a mental block roaming around your head. Three years ago, someone tried to disagree with this idea.

Lissy Beth said, "The Magic Wall forces people to believe that they only have one true talent. It is nonsense!"

So, is The Magic Wall true or fake? Let's find out. People insist that your attachment will be revealed in your palm if you are concentrating on these six things.

1. Concentrating on the moment

2. Hearing nature

3. Seeing everything from a mile away

4. Knowing everything you touch

5. Eating the thing you hate most

6. Smelling the Ghost of Doom

Matthew stopped reading at this point. He suddenly felt a net wrap around him. Was he going crazy? But the net was real, and it started to tighten. He realized it was actually a giant web. He had the article in his hand still and skimmed through it a few more times hoping to find a clue on what to do. Something led him to this room but maybe that something had left this article for him to find. Just when he thought he was losing the last glimmer of hope, something unbelievable happened. A gigantic spider jumped into room J. And who was riding on it?

"Ms. Teach!" yelled Matthew.

"Don't get too excited. Soon all of Magic World will be chasing after you. Assuming you can get out of this mess!" she laughed maniacally. "Have a good life, Daniel...Whatever is left of it. I hope you don't get bitten by Snuffles!" She disappeared.

The big spider started roaring. And now Matthew looked

closely and saw a rat standing on the spider. The rat grew bigger every second until its head hit the ceiling. Then the spider started lifting its legs and kicking it in the air.

"Um...I don't suppose you have learned your manners, have you?" asked Matthew sweetly. "I think we can be friends." The spider snarled. "I didn't say that in a mean way," he said quickly. Then the rat started chewing on his own claws. Matthew couldn't look. "You see, um...We can settle this. I don't like bullying animals. So, please just help me get out of here and I can do whatever you want. And I am hoping you understand English."

The rat nodded his head. He wrote something on the ground with his claws. It said, **"You're going to need our help to escape."**

Matthew shook his head. "I don't trust you."

"Then no escape" was the new message from the rat. Matthew started to yell as loudly as he could.

CHAPTER SEVEN

THE DAY THE BLACKOUT HITS

Terry sat down in his office. He had a lot to think about. Suddenly Mr. Fire came into Terry's room. Mr. Fire was frowning, and a tear rolled down his face. He said, "My brother is dead." Before Terry could react, he was gone.

Later that evening, Mr. Fire was sitting on his bed. He thought about the dying wish of his brother. His brother had said, "Find the Rainbow of Glee." He could not stop thinking about those words. "I'm sorry I had to abandon you, brother," he said holding up a picture of him. "You were alone when you died. You are a true teacher of Angora." He got a magic post-it note and wrote:

Dear Terry,
In this school, my heart only gets rained on by memories of my brother. I am sad to say hello to each and every one of my brother's beautiful students, knowing that the truth about his death would break their hearts. Some know him so well that they know the difference between me and him like the difference between you and Hornet. (I had to write that name to show my anger.) My heart is heavy carrying on my brother's dream to make it my own, but not finding joy in the process. So I am going to leave, searching for happiness.

From,
Fire the Second
p.s. Please do not try searching for me.

The magic post-it note walked into Terry's office.

Outside, everyone from group A and group B had lined up for the fight against the blackout. It would start like a tornado, but once it hit Angora, they were prepared for a blackout.

"For Angora!" yelled Ms. Angela. All the students repeated the phrase. "For Angora!"

* * *

Up in room J, Matthew was in desperate need of help. He pinched himself to see if he was dreaming. He whispered to himself, "Okay. I am trapped in a room with a giant monster, and I need its help to get out of here. I have to figure out what type of magician I am, and hopefully not be eaten by this giant."

So, Matthew went through the rules one by one. He first had to concentrate on the moment. He agreed with Lizzy Beth who said in the article that all of this was nonsense, but he had to try. He took a deep breath and focused. On the ground, the spider-rat observed him and wrote, **"This is not going to work**." But Matthew figured it was worth a shot. He felt calm and thought he had accomplished the goal of the first rule. Concentration.

"Rule 2 is that I have to hear nature. Now that is easy. I might not physically hear nature, but I know nature just said my plan is not going to work." The spider-rat gulped.

"Rule 3. Seeing everything from a mile away." The spider-rat wrote down, **"I can do that"** but Matthew had a thought. "You can't see anything clearly from a mile away, so I think the rule does not mean this literally. I think it means that when you're living in the present, you can visualize your future!" But that didn't really make sense. How could he see the future? **"People are preparing for the blackout battle"** wrote the creature suddenly. "Wait, what?" Matthew suddenly felt useless tied up in webs. Angora was preparing for war. Were they about to be crushed? Not that Matthew would do them any good, but he wanted to help. The creature stared curiously at him and wrote. **"What now?"**

"Okay, rat spider thing. Ms. Teach wanted me to be trapped here but I'm going to show her she's wrong." But how was he supposed to do that?

* * *

A new message popped up on Brown's phone and he smiled. This was an amazing breakthrough, a true connection between Magic and Non-Magic World. He walked into Terry's office and found Tom sitting there. "Oh, hello!"

Tom had been trying to avoid Brown but now didn't have a choice but to respond politely. "I fixed almost all the security cameras," Brown told Tom. "I wanted to watch this ad with the Principal because it may help him with his communication system. But maybe you can join me now." Tom shook his head showing he wasn't interested but Brown didn't notice and sat down next to him. He turned up the volume for the ad.

"Are you looking for a device unlike anything you've seen before? Then listen for more information on the Scuba Cube. The Scuba Cube is a special Rubik's cube with 6 faces, each divided into 9 unit-squares. When pressed, each of these smaller squares has a separate function. Get into the world of imagination and enjoy video games, different ways of communicating, and even ways to collaborate with friends on activities. You can link to your friends' Scuba Cubes to play a game. It is a world right at your fingertips, where you can get a break from regular life. So, for just $50,000 per Scuba Cube, it's all yours for a lifetime. Your hero, Jack, wants you to sit back and enjoy. There is no more driving to a shop to get groceries, just ask the Scuba Cube to get you your groceries, and it will turn it into an autopilot drone. Are you tired but cannot sleep? Ask it to compose a lullaby for you and you will be able to snooze quietly by yourself. Are you bored? Don't worry, my invention will be able to make you a best friend for you to spend time with! There are a few people we should thank who brought the Scuba Cube to life. Ms. Sharma and Mr. Daniel are top programmers who spent years working on this device. Act quickly and place your orders now!"

* * *

Terry was watching as group E started coming in to get prepped for battle. Only Matthew was still missing. "Poor Matthew," he whispered to himself. "What trouble is he in now?" Suddenly he spotted Fire the Second's post-it note waiting patiently on his desk. He read it a few times. "My heart is not full carrying on my brother's dream and making it my own," he read out loud. "He is comparing himself to Fire, and me to Hornet! He is going to search for happiness, away from the school. Is he going to the woods?" A tear rolled down his cheek as he realized Mr. Fire's body had been disposed of by Fire the Second without any celebration for his life. "I am sorry your life had to end this way, Fire!" said Terry. "I should have protected you. And when your brother came in with the news, I didn't know how to react. I am sorry."

* * *

Matthew had to now follow Rule 4. Knowing everything you touch. "That is impossible. For now, let's skip that one and go to Rule 5. I have to eat my least favorite thing." The spider-rat looked at him. "**I think you would hate to eat one of the things on my body.**" Matthew laughed. "That's so disgusting it's actually funny." But the spider-rat did not look amused. He started to cut off some of his skin. "No way! I am not eating that!" **"Then say goodbye to our help"** wrote the spider-rat.

Matthew felt helpless. The spider-rat stood patiently, and Matthew ate one little piece of the skin off its body. He felt like vomiting but swallowed quickly and grunted. "Okay. Next rule, smell the Ghost of Doom. Wait, the Ghost of Doom?"

"Oh no, not me" the spider wrote as the rat shook his head. **"No! You are not ready for the Ghost of Doom!"**

"What is the Ghost of Doom?" asked Matthew quietly.

The spider-rat hesitated then scribbled on the ground. **"The Ghost of Doom is the prince of nature. Karkatu is king. The Ghost of Doom controls a part of nature and commands it to follow its instructions. Apart from the Ghost of Doom, only special individuals called Nature Spirits can summon nature. Tori Nicholas is unfortunately a Nature Spirit. We need a competitor who is also a Nature Spirit who can stand up to her. The reason that Tori Nicholas** is so interested in me is that... I'm the Ghost of Doom. You saw how she was sitting on me. It's because I can control nature and she wants that power. But she needs the blood of another Nature Spirit as well as my blood to take over my powers."

Matthew looked confused. "Wait...Are you saying I'm trapped here because I'm a Nature Spirit? And this person – Tori Nicholas – who is she? I just saw Ms. Teach sitting on top of you." Suddenly the light bulb went off in his head. He rubbed his arm. "Wait, so Ms. Teach and Tori Nicholas are the same person? She's been using a fake name in Angora?" The spider-rat didn't respond.

Matthew started to look troubled. "How am I a Nature Spirit? I'm just a normal kid who doesn't care that much about nature."

The Ghost of Doom stood still for a few seconds then wrote **"You were chosen to be Ms. Teach's competitor. You will save Angora."**

Matthew shook his head in disbelief. "Who chose me? Why not Terry or Victoria or—"

The Ghost of Doom wrote faster than Matthew could think. **"You see, nature isn't unique to Magic World, it is in all the worlds. Your mission will be to not only bring nature to your side, but it will also be to unite Magic World and Non-Magic World. You will travel around each world on this mission, and you will succeed."**

"This is a lot for me to process," said Matthew. "I know the bullies drew my blood when they gave me that shot." The spider-rat nodded. "I don't understand how Ms. Teach and the bullies know I'm a Nature Spirit when I didn't know it myself."

He took a deep breath in and out. Suddenly, he realized there had been signs of his connection to nature, but he hadn't known what it meant. He thought of the vines and how they helped him with Alexander. "Wait, what does the article and rules have anything to do with this? The article was written by Tori Nicholas. That is Ms. Teach! Did she leave the piece of paper intentionally for me to find?"

"It was probably here from the time Ms. Teach arrived in Angora. You see, this paper is ancient, and it can never tear. The article changes every time you look at it, and it was hidden here. It is meant to lead you to understanding what type of spirit you are."

Matthew pursed his lips. "Still, I do not understand. Are you saying Ms. Teach wanted me to find out what type of spirit I was?"

The Ghost of Doom shook its head. "Ms. Teach underestimates you, Matthew. You see, she thought that we would not talk to each other at all. She thought that you would follow those steps on the article all by yourself. She wanted to mislead you and misguide you. I'm sure she set the first 5 steps up as a trap, a fake prophecy. If you did what it said, a cursed crystal would have pierced you, causing blood to streak down your skin."

Matthew shivered at the thought of blood oozing out of him. The Ghost of Doom went on, "So, Ms. Teach did not have any intentions of wanting you to find out who you really were. She wanted you to die here."

"Why should I believe you?" asked Matthew.

"Face it, you're more than just a normal kid, Matthew. You're a true Nature Spirit."

Matthew was confused. Was this strange animal speaking the truth? He focused and wiggled his toes and fingers, and at his command, the spider webs went away, and he was free. The door opened, signaling for him to leave.

"W-what was that?" asked Matthew, his breath shaky. He saw the response on the ground. **"The power of a real Nature Spirit."**

He nodded, still in shock. He had one more question. "Why are you called the Ghost of Doom?"

The Ghost of Doom hesitated then wrote, **"You see, Karkatu was doing an experiment with nature, combining plants and animals. Once, during a small experiment, Karkatu created me. Unfortunately, while I was evolving, there was a small family sitting down on a rock. Hopkins, Tori—"**

Matthew cut him off. "Wait, Hopkins and Tori – I mean Ms. Teach – were friends when they were kids?"

The Ghost of Doom nodded its head. **"They are more than that. They are sisters!"**

Matthew gasped, "Sisters!?"

"Ask Ms. Hopkins when you see her. Hopkins, Tori, their mother, and father were in the place where I was being created. And there was an accident...One of the parents died. I do not know how, but I know one of them died because of me and how I was created. After that, Ms. Teach despised Karkatu, and Karkatu blamed me for that. Ms. Teach then decided to become the new Ghost of Doom. She wants to destroy nature step by step, though it is a bit ironic since she is a Nature Spirit. After that, Karkatu called me the Ghost of

Doom since I was associated with death. He banished me from his circle."

"Can you join my crew then? I don't think what happened to you is fair. Angora might not think that they need your help, but they really do," Matthew pleaded, looking at the Ghost of Doom with respect. The Ghost of Doom paused then wrote **"Yes."** They walked out together.

* * *

The troops were lined up on the battlefield. "For Angora!" they chanted. The Principal left his room and went down to the battlefield. Mr. and Mrs. Daniel entered Terry's office a few minutes later. They wanted to see if anyone had news about Matthew.

Mrs. Daniel looked around wondering where Terry could be. But Mr. Daniel was frozen in place, staring at something glittering and sticking out of a drawer Terry had probably left open by mistake. The stone!

He moved closer and could see a post-it note jumping around the stone. "What's this?" he said and grabbed the note. "Ms. Hopkins and Matthew retrieved the stone from Non-Magic World."

"This is the same stone," Mr. Daniel said, amazed. He picked up the stone and turned it around in his hand. "Beautiful..." he said, still mesmerized by the artifact. "But this belongs to us," he continued. "Matthew took it from our bank locker for some reason."

"Matthew gave it to Magic World?" asked Mrs. Daniel, surprised. Mr. Daniel nodded sadly. He heard footsteps approaching. His instincts told him to throw the stone to Mrs. Daniel. "Hide it," he told her, tossing the stone gently to her. But Mrs. Daniel was too scared to catch it. It dropped on the floor and broke into two pieces. A light shined from both of them Mr. Daniels rushed to pick it up and shoved it back into the drawer along with the post-it note, regretting what had just happened.

Outside, Terry was waiting with the kids for the blackout. "It's going to be coming soon. Prepare your bows and arrows. Last time this happened the dark force came out. I do not know what will happen this time. But we have to position our weapons so that they won't misfire. We must hit our target." Everyone cheered.

The Daniels went outside and found Terry. "Do you think we are going to win this battle?" asked Mr. Daniel. "Even if we find Matthew, will it be safe for him?"

Terry responded, "The villains might overpower us, but we do have an ultimate weapon – the magic stone." Mr. and Mrs. Daniel looked at each other worried. "What's so special about this stone?"

"This stone is our key to defeating Ms. Teach," Terry explained. "It's the only way to keep all of us, including Matthew, safe. " The students called out to Terry, and he ran off to join them.

Now Mr. Daniel was very worried for Matthew's safety. "What will happen once Terry sees the stone is broken?" whispered Mrs. Daniel. "We have to do something."

Mr. Daniel quietly pulled out his Scuba Cube from his pocket. There was only one place they knew where they could find more stones and one person who could help them. It seemed to be the only way to make sure their son could survive.

* * *

Ms. Goliath was teaching a science class in the school. Melissa noticed Adam looking at his phone secretly, then he walked up to Ms. Goliath to tell her something and she allowed him to leave the room. Melissa also waved her hands and winked at her friends who did the same.

"What Melissa?" asked Ms. Goliath.

"We all have to use the bathroom."

Goliath looked suspicious. "All of you?"

Melissa nodded. "Maybe it's something we ate in the cafeteria."

She sighed and permitted them to leave.

"Come on, guys, let's follow Adam," said Melissa. Emily blinked her eyes. "Why?"

Melissa chuckled. "It is the perfect way to start testing out the new Scuba Cube. Tracking Adam."

"Wow, how did you get one of those?" wondered Julie, amazed. "I thought they were sold out. And they're crazy expensive."

Melissa smirked. "I have my ways...And it helps to have Jack of Jack Company as my uncle." They followed Adam outside. Adam ran to the area of the playground that had been blocked off ever since Matthew went sliding down the pole. He went exactly where Matthew had gone before. Adam saw a pole. He had to climb across the monkey bars to get to it. Adam was scared but it was now or never. He started to go across the monkey bars and a few seconds later, Melissa started climbing up too. John also started moving across but then felt himself slip.

"Help!" yelled John. He reached over and grabbed Melissa for balance. Melissa screamed and tried to push him back.

Adam realized they were following him and decided he had no time to waste. He reached out and grabbed Melissa's Scuba Cube that had fallen on the ground. He pushed button 8 on face 2. Water sprayed out and hit Melissa and John. While they were distracted, Adam quickly got to the top of the pole and slid down. Suddenly, the ground below him disappeared and he found himself underground.

"I did it," he whispered to himself. "I'm standing where Matthew found the stone. What next?" Something glittering on the ground caught his eye. "The stones..." Adam reached down and picked one up. He was examining the stone when a man's deep voice came from behind where Adam was standing. He screamed and stepped back. Then, Adam saw a dark figure.

"Who is it?" he asked. The man sniffed. Adam could only make out his eyebrows which were twitching. "Finally! A breath of fresh air. Thank you for freeing me, Adam. In return, let me explain some things to you."

Adam tried to be brave. "Who are you and what do you want? How do you know my name?"

The man stepped closer. "Little non-magical boy, coming to my domain and asking me questions. I should be asking you that question. But please, I am weak. Offer me a place to rest in your house. Just for an hour or two."

Adam shook his head. "You're crazy," he whispered.

As he stepped forward, Adam saw the man's expression.

"You don't understand. I once betrayed someone, or he betrayed me. Then I was cursed. And I, who used to be a champion, had to be imprisoned. That is, until you came along."

Adam didn't know what to say. Could he trust this person? He thought best to be sympathetic. "My dad, he died after he hid something. My mother cries about it every day. We all have problems."

"Well, I can help you get answers," said the stranger so seriously and with so much confidence that Adam almost believed him. "I can tell you about Justin."

Adam gasped. That was his father's name. "Who are you? How do you know about my family?"

"I met your dad when I was about your age. Trust me, I can answer all your questions and tell you everything you need to know. Can you help me?" The stranger spoke in a low raspy voice, like it hadn't been used in a long time.

"If I help you, I need you to promise me you'll tell me everything about my dad."

The man nodded. He had red eyes and was covered in dirt. It was hard to see his face clearly. Adam could tell he had a cloak on. He decided it was worth taking a risk to see if he and the stranger could help each other. Adam followed him as he took a different way out of the area, away from Melissa and her friends. He looked at the shiny stone in his hand and quietly put it in his pocket.

* * *

As the blackout started to rise, the sun started to set. "What is our strategy?" asked Tom. The Principal frowned. Suddenly they heard a loud THUMP! Matthew came into the room, the Ghost of Doom following behind. Terry jumped back and whimpered as he saw the giant beast.

Tom went up to Matthew. "Where were you?" he asked. Matthew reassured everyone that he was okay and that the Ghost of Doom was not evil. Terry updated Matthew on the blackout. He looked out the window and saw that Terry was right. It was dark and gloomy, like there was about to be a huge thunderstorm. He saw Victoria in the crowd. Then, the war started!

BOOM BAAM BOOM BAAM! Bombs started dropping. Matthew had never heard a bomb drop, but he never expected them to be this loud. The teachers of Angora had a few shields up in the air that blocked them from the bombs, but the shields would not hold forever. Matthew and Tom ran to Victoria.

"Matthew," she said, surprised to see him there. Matthew quickly explained to Victoria what happened. "I can't believe Ms. Teach wanted you dead," mumbled Victoria. "I knew we should have never trusted her."

Matthew nodded agreeingly. More bombs scattered. Ms. Angela was giving encouraging comments to the kids. "You will do great on the battlefield," she cheered.

Then Terry squawked, "War!" A few sixth-grade kids started to charge, holding up their shields. More giant cannonballs came soaring.

"Defend!" screamed Angela. But Terry thought differently.

"Attack back with our cannonballs." Everyone cheered. They jumped on horses and each of them got cannonballs. The cannonballs were not big, they started out small, but when you threw them, they became bigger. Even Matthew jumped on some random horse. He got a cannonball to fire. Terry noticed some enemies crossing the line and getting into Angora. "Charge!" he ordered confidently. A few people on the enemies' side ran as fast as they could with their swords drawn. "Get them!" Terry howled at many people on the battlefield. They all charged at the enemies, bringing them down with their swords. But Terry saw that more and more people were crossing the Angora line. "Reinforcements!" he now screeched.

Brown came up to Terry in a hurry. "I feel something big," he said.

Terry raised an eyebrow. "What do you mean by big?"

Brown shrugged. "Some animal, I think, but at the same time it seems human too. I'm detecting it on my radar, but I can't see clearly. Is there something half-animal and half-human?" Terry ignored Brown and gulped. Ms. Teach was coming.

Matthew galloped away on his horse after he launched a cannonball into the air. "YAAA!" he yelled. After everyone had fired the cannonballs, their enemies unfortunately came back with more ammunition. The cannonballs came rushing at the speed of light, and a sound like a strong wind howling.

"Retreat to home base!" roared Angela, but Terry glared at her.

"Are you kidding? Retreating will just clear the way for them so they get into our school easily. We are not retreating. We're going to fight until we win!"

Victoria shook her head. "We can't let them see us weak. Retreating would be our best bet right now so we have time to come up with a new strategy."

Terry laughed at this. "Excuse me, Victoria. Do you think you have more experience than the Principal of Angora?"

Victoria shook her head. "I am not stronger or more experienced than you, but I think I am smarter in this case." Terry looked shocked at her response.

He spoke up. "In chess, there is a reason why the pawns can't move back a space. There is a reason why the king doesn't retreat easily—"

"Unless he is the only one standing," said Victoria, cutting him off. "There is a reason half the pieces can move back! It's about positioning yourself for a win."

The Principal looked embarrassed. "Fine! I'll let some kids be removed from battle and put into the training center. But once the blackout hits—"

The rest of his sentence was drowned out by a loud noise. BOOM!

"What just happened?" wondered Matthew. It didn't look like any damage had been done, but then he realized what had made the loud noise. A giant spider and rat were approaching. They looked different from the one he had seen just a little while ago.

"Is this the second Ghost of Doom? Or the third? What are

we in for," he whispered to himself.

* * *

While those on the battlelines were looking uneasily at the spider and rat, back in Non-Magic World, Adam entered his house with the strange man behind him, and a strange stone in his pocket. His house was at the top of Rosemary Hill. It looked like a crooked mansion. He was still holding Melissa's Scuba Cube in his hand, in case of an emergency.

Goliath ran into the foyer when she heard his footsteps. "Adam! What happened to you? Where were you?" she stopped talking when she saw the man with Adam and stared.

"Hornet – is that you? I can't believe it. We thought you were dead. You've been missing for years."

Hornet gave her an evil stare then glanced at Adam. "Your mother, she is a smart woman, but she has been hiding a lot from you."

Adam looked confused. "You know each other? What's going on?"

"This man is dangerous, Adam," stated Goliath. "Step towards me."

Hornet took a deep breath. "I am sorry I have to do this so soon after meeting you, Adam." He held up his hand and a rope appeared. He lassoed Adam and the next second, Adam was tied up in ropes.

Goliath screeched. She pulled out her Scuba Cube and said: "Call police!" Suddenly, she heard a robotic voice say: "Request accepted."

Within a minute, two police officers came in, armed with guns. "What is it, Goliath?" they asked. Hornet smiled, and then turned his fist. The two police officer started to hit each other, and then suddenly, their eyes turned completely white. Goliath gasped.

"Arrest that boy!" Hornet wailed. "He tried to rob me!"

Goliath shivered; she did not know if they were going to follow his command. They did. They turned to Adam and picked him up.

"Let me go!" Adam yelled. "Mom!"

Goliath rushed forward to stop them. "What are you doing? I'm commanding you to stop." But the police officers looked like robots completing a task. One of them quickly handcuffed Goliath to the railing of the staircase so she couldn't move.

Hornet moved closer to Adam. "Give me the stone. I know you are hiding it in your pocket."

Adam laughed hoping he sounded brave. "Very funny! I have nothing. You don't scare me." The man moved even closer to Adam. "Why are the police here listening to you?" Adam wondered. "Why aren't they following my mom's orders?"

The man laughed. He could read Adam's mind. "Because I am Hornet! The master of the mind! But you are a tough one to tackle, Adam. Because you have a few things of your own on your mind."

* * *

The new Ghost of Doom had arrived, and it was monstrous.

"Attack!" yelled Terry.

Bow and arrows were brought into position. "Now!" ordered Terry when he had seen the rat's tail. Rainbow colored arrows went flying at the rat.

"No way can it withstand that. Even being the Ghost of Doom, I don't think any of the arrows are going to miss. We have a perfect angle to fire because the rat has turned his back. I would say looking at the way the arrows are going, in about 2 seconds the Ghost of Doom will fall!" predicted Victoria. Unfortunately, she was wrong. The rat and spider just turned invisible, and after that, people who looked like zombies came charging towards them.

Terry needed to boost everyone's confidence. "TO ANGORA!!!" he chanted at the top of his voice. But nobody repeated after him. "I said - TO ANGORA! " Again, nobody answered. They were busy staring at the zombies. Soon their eyes started to glow red. Even Victoria and Tom's eyes turned red. It was creepy.

"What is happening?" wondered Matthew, shaken. Then a burst of light came from the sun. He thought this was supposed to be a blackout. Suddenly he realized the sun seemed to be exploding.

He shielded his eyes and decided to run back into the school. He had a nagging feeling he was needed inside. As soon as Matthew ran in, he saw a knife being pointed at the original Ghost of Doom. Holding the knife was Ms. Teach. The door behind him shut and Matthew knew he couldn't escape. He started to piece together everything.

"You want to be the original Ghost of Doom," he guessed. "That's why you keep trying to overpower the spider-rat here."

Ms. Teach laughed. "Took you long enough to realize that. I can now command nature, Matthew. Imagine how powerful I'll be in the truest form of the original Ghost of Doom. You may be a Nature Spirit but I'm one level above you. And soon, our Mind Master Hornet will arrive to destroy your home. He's already awakened and has your friend Adam in his possession."

Matthew looked up at Ms. Teach. "Kill me, but don't touch anybody else in Magic and Non-Magic worlds," he said quietly. "Deal?"

Ms. Teach laughed again. "No deal. I can kill you right now and do whatever I want after." But that was when the Ghost of Doom caught her foot and she tripped.

"You are a traitor! All of nature will laugh into your shabby face!" wrote the original Ghost of Doom. Ms. Teach punched the ground with her fists and then, something unbelievable happened. She turned into a giant Ghost of Doom like the one Matthew had just seen outside in the battlefield.

Matthew's heart was racing but he didn't react.

The original Ghost of Doom looked furious. "How dare you treat another Nature Spirit this way?" he said in a human-like voice. He was about to slash Ms. Teach with his sharp claws when she turned invisible.

"You can speak?" Matthew asked the spider-rat, both relieved and surprised.

The spider-rat smiled and was about to say something when he suddenly toppled over backwards. "Ms. Teach is still here. She's invisible and attacking me." The rat seemed to be choking and the spider appeared frozen. Matthew looked around the room for a weapon. The only interesting thing he found in his room was the magic post-its. But those wouldn't help. Then he noticed something sparkling in the air. Although Ms. Teach was invisible, her necklace wasn't. He recognized it to be Ms. Hopkin's necklace, the one that was found in Mr. Simon's room.

"I can't believe you stole her necklace," whispered Matthew. He grunted in disgust at Ms. Teach. The spider-rat had also noticed the necklace at this point and was trying to pounce on it, hoping to catch Ms. Teach. Matthew heard another boom from outside and felt the urge to get back into battle. But he could not abandon Sprat – the name of the spider and rat which came into his mind at that moment. It seemed to be on his side and was trying to protect him. He grabbed a magic post-it and wrote a note to Ms. Hopkins: Ms. Teach is in room E. The original Ghost of Doom is in danger. Find her and stop her.

The post-it note sprang into action and floated out of the room towards Ms. Hopkins. Matthew ran back downstairs, noticing that weirdly some people's eyes were now normal, and some were still red. The sun seemed to continue exploding.

"Angora will soon turn into dust!" predicted Terry.

Matthew found Tom and Victoria and told them what was going on inside. He hoped Ms. Hopkins would be safe facing Ms. Teach. But their priority was the exploding sun.

"Have any ideas?" asked Matthew. He expected Victoria to

raise her hand and say, "Yes, I do," like she usually did in class, but this time she was quiet.

Ms. Hopkins, meanwhile, received Matthew's message and charged into the group E room. Ms. Teach was still there being held down by Sprat. She was back to being visible now.

"LET ME GO!" she screamed as Ms. Hopkins' face bubbled with confusion.

Ms. Teach looked half-human and half-animal. She was trying to morph into her Ghost of Doom form, but Sprat was holding her arms back.

Ms. Hopkins was not confident she could deal with Ms. Teach. "Should I call the guards?" she wondered aloud.

Ms. Teach laughed hard. "I can kill them with a snap of my fingers!"

Ms. Hopkins looked terrified. "Why are you doing this sister?" she asked in a scared tone as Ms. Teach laughed hysterically.

"Why would I tell you my plan?" responded Ms. Teach.

And that was when Ms. Hopkins saw the necklace around Ms. Teach's neck. She yelped. "You monster! You used my necklace to turn into a Ghost of Doom?"

Ms. Teach sighed. "I think you have just gotten too emotional, Ms. Hopkins."

* * *

Outside, Victoria had been quietly thinking through the chaos. She had a plan. Tom shook his head when she shared her thoughts. "No! I am not some ballerina who will dance to your plans."

Victoria pleaded with him. "This is sure to work!"

Matthew did not know what to say. "Just to clarify – you want us to fly up to the sun? That too an exploding sun? I want to make sure I didn't misunderstand."

"Trust me. This will work. But we only have an hour," yelled Victoria, seeing the yellow ball of fire get closer to Angora.

"I have two pairs of magic goggles. You and Tom take them. I can go to Ms. Hopkins to help her."

Matthew nodded. If they were going to die anyway as the scorching sun got near them, he may as well try to do something about it. But he wished they had more protection. He looked up at the sun with his magic goggles.

"Um... Maybe I forgot but did Victoria mention how we are going to get to the sun? Are we taking a rocket ship?"

Tom chuckled. "I can help out with that!" He held up his wand and in the next few seconds they were up in the air on a big cloud. "There are actually two suns. One is for Magic World, the other for Non-Magic World. Our sun has different properties though. The sweat or water that we produce in Magic World will evaporate and get absorbed into the sun. They don't form clouds. We are on a rare cloud that made its way into our atmosphere. The sun will not produce water that rains down on us. Instead, the sun will rain down fire bolts that produce water if you use the churning machine. In some bad cases, any clouds that float here from Non-Magic World can get intercepted by the sun and go, KABOOM! They explode! I wonder how many of your buddies have exploded?" Tom asked the cloud.

The cloud just whimpered.

"Wait – did the cloud just respond to you? What is going on? And why are we on a cloud if it could explode?" asked Matthew frantically.

"Well, when items from Non-Magic World end up in Magic World, they sometimes take on magical properties," replied Tom like it was totally normal.

Matthew nodded as though this made sense.

By this time, they had reached Mercury. Tom did a somersault off the cloud and started to float in the air. Matthew also hopped off the cloud to join Tom, and it was just in time. He saw the poor cloud explode and he suddenly felt hatred for Ms. Teach. She had caused so much destruction. Matthew could not control where he was floating, and they both started to crash land into the sun.

"WHOA!" screamed Matthew. Tom tried to steady himself but felt dizzy with the bright light and heat. He fell to the ground.

* * *

Down in Magic World, Terry was destroying bombs with his bare hands. He was losing energy and getting tired and grumpy. Suddenly, Terry started breathing fire and zapping lightning. "YAA!" he yelled loudly. Images of a man with a black cloak popped up in his mind, along with the word "revenge".

"I hate people," Terry shouted. "Yeah!"

Everybody started to move away from Terry. "If Angora falls, the whole world will be destroyed!" he continued to scream.

A big giant walked towards Terry who killed him in one shot. The teachers were both in awe as well as scared of Terry. He kept fighting until there was no monster left to fight.

"We won!" someone shouted, and everyone cheered. Terry made his way to the school stage and spoke into the microphone.

"We have won for now. But we have a lot of work left to do. There is an exploding sun – we will be destroyed unless someone takes care of it. Also, we do not know who Ms. Teach is working for, but it must be someone powerful. Right now, we have a lot of cleaning up to do and need to vacate the area to assess the damage. Teachers, go to room E."

Meanwhile, up in the air, when Matthew and Tom landed on the sun, Tom thought it felt the same as the Non-Magic World sun. He looked over at Matthew who seemed anxious.

"Matthew! Is this your first time on the sun?"

"Of course!" Matthew yelled. "What did you think?"

Tom shrugged. "The first time I flew up to the sun—"

"You've been to the sun already and didn't think to tell me?! I was so freaked out because I thought nobody had ever done this before."

Tom took a deep breath. He started singing a song. "If you are sca-red—"

Matthew practically had smoke coming out of his ears.

Then Tom said, "Well, I thought of Mr. Fire. He is not really scared of much, even though he was once almost eaten by a jaguar."

"That's an inspiring story Tom, but right now—"

Tom interrupted, "I get it. We need to focus on the main problem. Let's get on with the plan before those ugly monster lava guys come!"

Matthew grunted in frustration. "Lava guys. Great."

"Oh yeah, I forgot to mention," Tom continued. "I think we are right next to a lava pool." And Tom was sure right.

Matthew gulped. "This is the worst day of my life!" First, a crab came out of the lava. "Okay. It is just a crab! Let's go!"

But Tom was examining it. "Fascinating! I need it for one of my experiments." He made a jar appear and lured the crab into it.

Matthew was annoyed. "Quick, you are just wasting time. We have to stop the sun from exploding!"

"As you should know, if you had paid attention to the plans, this is what I'm trying to do. These animals will be an amazing source of help!"

Matthew took a deep breath in and apologized. "I just want to get back safe and sound."

Tom nodded understandingly as he and Matthew started to walk to the right. But they did not know what they were getting themselves into. They were heading into deep trouble and had no clue.

* * *

Goliath ran into Melissa's house. "Your father is back! Where is your mother? He's taken my Adam with him." Tears were running down her face.

Melissa laughed. "Have you gone crazy? My dad is dead."

Goliath shook her head. "You do not understand, Melissa. He is back and dangerous. We were trying to protect you. And now my precious Adam—" she sobbed.

Suddenly, blue flames came out of Melissa's hands. Streaks of lightning! She screamed. "I don't understand - get this off me. What is happening!"

Goliath's eyes widened. "It's the beginning. He is transferring some of his powers to you. I was afraid this would happen one day. Listen to me carefully. There isn't too much I can tell you right now. But trust me on this. Soon, you will be able to choose your path, Hornet or—"

But Melissa didn't stop to listen to the rest of her sentence. She was terrified and ran out of the room to find her mother.

A few hours later, a transmission was sent to everyone's phone. A man was standing in the middle of the screen. He was dressed in armor, as though there was a dragon about to attack. He had brown skin and white hair. He had eyes as dark as a back bear's fur, and he looked as scared as a lost puppy.

"Well... I am the guard to the most powerful man in the world. My name is Leroy. Let me present to you, Jack Pierce!"

A man with headphones came on. Jack gave a smirk. "My message is meant for the whole world. First, a round of applause. Jack the Great! I started my company with just a small band of workers. And then I grew and grew, building my own brand. So next, let's give a shout out to the Jack Company. Finally, let us expand the business. Everyone around the world, this is your chance to be a millionaire.

Buy a Scuba Cube and you will be helping yourself. We are going to add—"

Melissa turned off her screen. She was confused and upset as she called her mom. "Where are you? I've been trying to find you. You lied about everything! You never told me my dad was some – magician or wizard who went missing. All my life I thought my dad was dead. So, no matter what you say, I will get answers from Uncle Jack today."

She hung up the phone as she went to meet her friends. John heard Melissa's update and did not know how to make her feel better. "Your mom is so bad, Melissa! In fact, maybe she is as bad as your brother."

Melissa made a weird face. "Um... John, I don't have a brother. But you, Emily, and Joanne are like siblings to me. We stick together. And I have a prank for us to play." The others looked up at her, curious to see what she had in mind.

"All of my bad luck started with Matthew. He's up to something and it's made my dad come back from the dead – but I don't even know who he is, and Ms. Goliath claims he is evil. I now have strange powers, and everything in my life seems to have changed. Matthew has to pay for this. We are going to set the Daniels' house on fire!"

CHAPTER EIGHT

A BUMP AND SOME HEAT

Hornet looked right into Adam's eyes like a bald eagle eyeing its prey. He zoomed into the little boy's face, not paying attention to anyone else. Adam was scared out of his mind. He did not know what to do.

"Many of us have a back story that is full of sadness. Do you know why I am like this, Adam? I'd like to share the story with you one day," said Hornet. "But first, you need to know your own story."

Adam suddenly saw a vision. Hornet and a boy were walking on the sidewalk. "Terry, I am going to be a master chess player!" bellowed Hornet as if he was a king. Terry smiled. They walked into a house which had a name plate outside its door. The plate had the letters **C o t m. H n. S e f a m a. K e y t. E t y h m. S t g o t w.** When they opened the door, they realized it was an empty house, and then a bunny came in. But this bunny was different. It had fangs the size of a monster. Terry stared at it in shock. It pounced on Terry who tried to fight back, but the bunny dug his teeth right into Terry's skin.

Terry screamed in pain and agony, "Help me, Hornet!"

"See you later or never!" snickered Hornet.

Adam's vision ended and he started to cough. He felt sympathy for Terry, a lot of it.

Hornet spoke. "Adam, you saw the little boy named Terry? You felt sorry for him? Because of him, your father is lost, lost in a crystal."

* * *

Meanwhile, Ms. Hopkins was standing with her wand facing Ms. Teach. Tears fell from her eyes. "I thought that I could trust you sister! Because now I know what is really in your heart. What you want is war!"

Ms. Teach gave an evil grin as Sprat started to lose its grip on her.

"Hopkins, what are you doing just standing there? Come and help me. We are sisters after all." Ms. Teach started shooting arrows out of her mouth. "I love this day! The day I rise up more than anyone in the whole entire world!"

She untangled herself from Sprat and punched Ms. Hopkins on the right side of her mouth. Ms. Hopkins felt numb. Sprat kicked Ms. Teach as hard as it could, seeing destruction everywhere. Bricks were falling, just missing their heads. Sprat then saw one falling towards them like a rocket ship, and it was about to hit Ms. Hopkins.

"Watch out!" it yelled. Ms. Hopkins looked above her and saw the brick. She jumped out of the way, and it hit Ms. Teach who grunted but then just got right back up.

"You don't understand the difference between good and bad!" she screamed as she rammed into Ms. Hopkins. Ms. Teach was looking right into her eyes as though motioning that she was going to kill her.

"If you want a fight, just say it, because I want one." And it took some time for Ms. Teach to register that Ms. Hopkins was saying that.

Ms. Teach snickered, "Your necklace might want a fight!" The necklace started to hit Ms. Hopkins. "If I control the Ghost of Doom, I control nature! And I think your necklace is being controlled by me. Isn't that your Heart of Magic?"

The sun was exploding faster, and rain started flooding Angora. Ms. Teach was about to break the necklace when something started pulling her tail in her Ghost of Doom form. She looked behind her and saw Victoria.

"No!" yelled Ms. Teach. Victoria gave her a dirty look and howled, "Sorry Ms. Teach, but how about you stop bullying Ms. Hopkins and give up? Try something new."

Ms. Teach shook her head. "Never!" she bellowed furiously.

Ms. Hopkins smiled at her. "Then maybe we should do this the hard way." Sprat bit Ms. Teach's legs. CRICK! Ms. Teach fell, but it was not much time until she got back up. "Maybe you are my first kill, original Ghost of Doom, so that I can really control all of nature!" she started laughing deliriously.

* * *

At that very moment, Matthew and Tom were seeing weird things. A pot of glue, and a yellow pencil. Tom looked scared. "As you know, this is not like the Non-Magical sun, so these items won't burn."

Matthew looked serious. "Really, I think we should step away!" And so, they ran off to explore another part of the sun. "There must be animals around here somewhere!" Tom said. He looked around and saw a small cave. "Hmm... maybe in there."

Matthew could tell this cave was not naturally formed. There was nothing special inside, just some black fur spread all over the floor. Tom now regretted that they walked into the cave and was about to suggest they leave. Suddenly, a lava monster appeared, and the ground started spinning fast! The cave door shut, and lava started to spray everywhere.

"Now we are dead!" Matthew said unenthusiastically.

The monster did not look too friendly. His eye sockets were big holes, and he did not have a nose or ears. He was orange.

"If we can step on the sun, won't it be a breeze to step on the lava monster?" asked Matthew anxiously, but to his disappointment, Tom shook his head.

"Matthew, I would say if we had to die, we should jump into the lava monster headfirst! It is always the least painful way, and the coolest way," Tom said with confidence.

Matthew tried to gulp down his fears. "Unfortunately, with Tom around there's always something to fear," he thought to himself.

"Oh yeah, I forgot to mention that we anyway die if we stay up here for another 45 minutes, so we have to solve the problem and get back to Magic World."

Matthew put on his "Great To Know" look. Suddenly, he thought he spotted an exit at the back of the cave, but it was just a dead end. And right there was a second blob of lava.

"Oh no," said Tom, looking away from it. "We were being

chased by the female blob of lava. This is the male!"

The female came closer and made some strange sounds. Matthew realized he could understand her. "Kill them! They hurt me in the eye!" she said as the male came forward.

"Intruders!" he yelled as he swerved his lava tail. Tom and Matthew dodged it.

"We only have 50% of our oxygen left!" commented Tom. "There is no hope that we can get out of here in 30 minutes."

"Why did we ever think we could do anything about the exploding sun?" Matthew wondered. The only thing he saw made the situation more complicated. Eggs that were about to hatch. "We are about to be in a lava parade!" he remarked.

The male lava monster laughed. "You won't see that in time. Because for their first hunting practice, they will eat you!"

Tom tried running away but the female blob put her tail right in front of them. "Not one more step!" she said. Matthew tried to stay calm to figure a way out of this mess. There was only one thing they had with them - a crab. This gave Matthew an idea. He took the jar from Tom and released the crab.

"We are not evil! We just rescue animals that we see around us from blobs like you."

But the male blob chuckled. "Animals like these live in the sand—" He stopped and looked at the crab who appeared very grumpy. "Oh no! You boys do not know who this is, do you? This is no ordinary crab. Listen, Mr. Crab, I am so sorry that I did not invite you to the party." He started hitting himself as the crab watched, amused. Then the crab waltzed over to the female blob and started pinching her.

"Ow-Ow!" she screamed. And when the male blob came to rescue her, a thousand more crabs appeared and started pinching them. Matthew and Tom decided not to wait around and see how this would end.

"That is what they deserve," said Matthew, happy that luck was on their side.

"Now, let's get out of here!" replied Tom, until he realized the only exit was covered with lava and crabs. "Looks like we have to do this the hard way." He looked at Matthew wondering how to tell him they had to crash through the monsters and crabs and hope for the best. Matthew though calmly raised his arms and a good block of lava started to move. Now they had a clear path to the exit.

Tom was confused. "How did you do that?" He was quiet for a few seconds. "You're a Nature Spirit?" he whispered.

Matthew nodded. "Come on."

They exited the cave and followed a path to their right which brought them to an area with a small body of bubbling water. "This looks like the Magnetic Bowl which keeps the sun hot and intact. It's a powerful magnet but it's dangerous if its off balance."

Matthew looked puzzled. "How do we know if its off-balance?"

"Because of where that rock is," replied Tom. He pointed to a large shiny rock that was the magnetic core of the sun. "We need to move it into the bowl for the sun to stop exploding. But the catch is, we can't touch it, or we'll burn to death."

Tom raised his wand and closed his eyes. "Let's hope I get this spell right... Kola!" Immediately the rock core lifted up and moved towards the bowl. Suddenly, Tom's arm felt weak, and his wand slipped down a little. The rock slid into the side of the bowl and rested on the edge.

The sun turned black.

"What happened?" exclaimed Matthew, shivering and already wanting more light. He heard a few cries as he tried to find Tom in the dark. He held Tom's hand so they wouldn't get separated and started to move around, bumping into many things.

An alarm sounded. "Oxygen level at 25%," Tom said quietly. "I messed up. The rock can't touch the edge of the bowl, it has to be right in the middle. Now we're stuck in the dark as well as everyone else on Magic World. This is a disaster."

Matthew did not know what to say. First, they were in an exploding sun trying to get it to stop, and now they were in a different kind of blackout. A small flickering light caught his eye. It was moving towards him.

"What's that?" he asked in a hushed tone. Tom started at it. "Unbelievable...It's a sun-lob. Rare creatures that have a magnetic force and glow in the dark. It's attracted to you."

"Do you think it's because I'm a Nature Spirit? I feel something pulling me towards it too."

The sun-lob started to climb up Matthew. "This might be our solution," said Tom. "The sun-lob can move the rock for us! Gently place it near the rock and give it a push. It might be small but it's powerful enough to move anything that's magnetic. But make sure you don't touch the rock itself."

"Easy task," muttered Matthew sarcastically. He very carefully lifted up the sun-lob and placed it next to the rock. The sub-lob froze for a few seconds then glowed more brightly. They saw it moving in the water.

"I think it's working," exclaimed Tom. He didn't realize he had been holding his breath. A minute later, the light stopped in the middle of the bowl. Immediately, it was bright everywhere. Just then, Matthew felt himself getting drowsy. He was about to fall when Tom pulled him back up. Matthew opened his eyes and blinked rapidly. The sun was back to normal. Neither black nor exploding.

"What happened?" he asked Tom.

"Quick, we can talk about everything later, but I think you blanked out for a few seconds. We only have 7% oxygen now." Matthew was still very confused but listened to Tom.

* * *

Jack was on the screen for everyone with a Scuba Cube to see. He had dark skin and blue eyes, white hair and had the same T-shirt as his assistant. He was quite short. As he got up, he started to talk. "As you know, our last invention, the Scuba Cube, was a smashing hit. It has made me a very wealthy man. But let me get to the point. You know how Antarctica is unclaimed, well, I want to occupy it, and destroy all that disgusting ice to build a giant factory. Maybe even a few factories. But I need your help. All of you, from kids to grownups. Call the Jack Store right now for further instructions. You can be a hero! Goodbye."

Brown was staring at his screen as though it was a piece of junk. "Er... First everything goes black, then it appears my iPad is back to working properly, and then I get to see the worst ad of all! Who would want to take over Antarctica? Jack of Jack Company will pay!" Brown crumpled lots of magic post-it notes out of frustration.

Mr. Daniel and Mrs. Daniel were looking out the window but could not see their son. "I hope Adam got the stone," said Mrs. Daniel. "If only there was something besides the stone that we could do to help!" she exclaimed.

* * *

Melissa was at the Daniels' house with John, Emily, and Joanne. "Now that I have lighting powers, it is better I use it." She kicked open the front door and it broke. Next, she shot lightning at all security cameras so no one could spot her.

She glanced at John, and they smiled at each other. "Nice shot Melissa!" he said enthusiastically.

Melissa walked around the house. "Steal everything that looks valuable. I will destroy everything else!" she added, zapping lightning at the chandeliers. She laughed in an evil way.

Suddenly, her eyes turned white. She heard a voice in her head. "Well done, my girl. I'm Hornet - your father. I can't reveal myself to you yet, but we will meet soon. Ask your grandmother for a yacht. Keep the mission quiet. We will make our way to Ecuador on June 21st." The voice in her head stopped and Melissa started breathing heavily. Did she imagine that? Something told her it was real. Her dad had spoken.

As she joined them, Melissa saw that her friends had loaded everything into a truck. They gave the truck drivers plenty of money to not spread the news of them stealing, and more money to drive them to Melissa's house. They unloaded everything into her basement where her mom rarely went, then drove over to Jack's house.

* * *

The heat was burning Matthew's toes, and the moon started twirling just a few thousand miles away from the sun. All because of Ms. Teach.

"Tom, hopefully when we turned off the magnetic core and then back on again, the sun went back to being normal!" But really,

Matthew had just jinxed it. Not everything was back to normal. A lava monster appeared from behind.

"I have been doing research about the sun my whole life, yet I don't know much about these lava monsters. They seem to be coming out of their caves. I wonder why!" yelled Tom, frustrated. But then they got their answer. The sun was getting colder and colder.

"Maybe they need a warmer home," guessed Matthew. "The temperature hasn't stabilized yet." As they watched, the lava monster jumped down from the sun (as it turned out, to Non-Magic World). Then more monsters came.

"Heat level – 43%, Oxygen level, 2%," read Tom looking down at his monitor.

Female lava monsters protected their eggs and watched as a few more monsters jumped down to Non-Magic World. Matthew looked out, trying to spot Magic World. He thought he could see it, a hot shade of pink on one half, and red like fire on the other. Matthew had a feeling it represented good and bad, but there was no way to find out unless he could make his way back. They were running out of oxygen. Only 1%. Matthew knew he was taking a giant risk but what other choice did he have? He signaled to Tom who nodded, with a serious expression. They both activated their magic vests and jumped straight down into Magic World.

* * *

Sprat started to dig its claws into Ms. Teach's skin, and she yelped. She could not teleport right now.

Ms. Hopkins stood close to her. "You knew the new location

of Angora so that you could tell your master! Who is your master?"

Ms. Teach was struggling out of the Ghost of Doom's claws. "Why would I tell you? Traitor you are, pure traitor!" She struggled to free herself and dodged each and every punch that Sprat was throwing at her. "I am going to destroy all of you, you have made the wrong choice. He is rising, I am rising!" screamed Ms. Teach.

"I cannot lose my grip!" Sprat exclaimed, and Ms. Hopkins could feel it straining. "Give the necklace to me!" said Ms. Hopkins and Sprat tossed it to her.

Ms. Hopkins safely put the necklace around her neck but "SPLOOCH!" The necklace made that exact noise as soon as Ms. Hopkins put it on herself. It twirled around her neck and hit her chest. She tried fiddling with it, to get it off, but it was useless. "What did you do?!" Ms. Hopkins asked furiously.

Ms. Teach chuckled. "It was all part of the plan, Ms. Hopkins. I am going to destroy you!" That was when they heard a "Splash!" A splash that was so powerful that everyone living in Magic World was able to hear it.

Matthew and Tom had landed in some water and were badly injured. They saw Angora in a distance, but blood was streaking down their legs, and they couldn't move. Matthew's mind was telling his body to do something. It was telling him to whistle. But Matthew figured that must be because he was so dizzy. He could barely move his hands, and he fell right to sleep.

* * *

An hour later he was woken up by a ticking sound. Tom was right next to Matthew. "Big fall we had!" he said. Matthew was so surprised to see Tom that he accidently kicked him.

"Ow!" yelled Tom, "I am so glad to see that you are okay, I was almost certain that you were dead. A magic doctor checked on us when Terry told her that we were down here, hurt. We both had many broken bones, and the doctor had to give us a very rare type of medicine called 'IKAWAWA' medicine. She will be relieved to hear that you are okay."

"Good to hear that you are well," said Matthew, and he patted Tom on the back. "Did we stop the sun from exploding?"

Tom nodded. "Yes! Everything went just as planned, except Angora apparently had a five-minute blackout at one point. Terry told me that everything just went...dark."

Matthew shrugged. "Is Angora safe and out of danger? Is Ms. Teach still around?" he asked.

Tom shook his head. "We don't know. Good news, many of the staff has escaped Angora and are in a safe location. Bad news, we have no record of Ms. Hopkins, Victoria, and all the other students. They're probably still in Angora fighting. We just have to hope that they will win."

* * *

Victoria tried scratching Ms. Teach once Sprat lost its grip. "You idiot girl. I wish you were dead!" yelled Ms. Teach to Victoria, but Victoria didn't care and charged at her. Ms. Teach grunted and the spider came down from her head, distracting Victoria. Ms. Teach pushed her to the ground and said, "Good! That should take care of her."

She looked at the original Ghost of Doom and started ramming into him. The Ghost of Doom fell to the ground, gasping for breath. Ms. Teach was now facing Ms. Hopkins. "Okay! One on one once more, what do you say?"

Ms. Hopkins tried kicking Ms. Teach, but Ms. Teach simply pulled her leg and threw her on the ground. "Your time is over Ms. Hopkins!"

Suddenly, Sprat got back up and punched Ms. Teach. "Ahhh!" she cried in pain. Ms. Hopkins pulled out her wand. "Escarpment!" she managed to yell.

"Oh no," thought Ms. Teach. She turned back into human form and realized that she would be overpowered soon. "Don't think this is over," she said menacingly. In a swift moment she teleported away.

Ms. Hopkins went over to Victoria. "Thanga!" she whispered, and Victoria was up on her feet. She lightly gazed at Ms. Hopkins, then Sprat. "Thank you! Wow, both of you look horrible. Hope you aren't in too much pain."

The sun was starting to set. "We have to contact Terry," Ms. Hopkins said anxiously. "We have five minutes to change the location of Angora. Or we risk Ms. Teach coming back with a vengeance."

Meanwhile, Terry was sitting next to Matthew. Tom updated him on what had happened on the sun. "I'm very proud of both of you. You've saved Angora and all of Magic World. I might have been a bit hard on everyone in the school, Matthew. Especially during this battle! But I want to apologize. Do you accept my apology? Quick!

Hurry up and answer me boy!"

Matthew smiled and nodded his head. "You in particular, have to be careful from now on. It's clear that Ms. Teach is after you. We haven't prepared you enough for this situation," Terry explained.

"Magic is not judged by how many spells you know," he continued. "That is why until 6th grade we do no spells. What magic is judged on is how you use your spells. Did you know that with every spell you use, you get a tiny bit weaker? There are two spells though that do not make you weaker. No one knows why. Do you want to learn them?"

Matthew was amazed to hear this. "Yes."

"Okay. You will need this spell to light up the dark. This would have been helpful when it was dark on the sun. It is the spell of light. It does no harm unless you command it to. This spell might not be an extraordinary spell, but as a beginner, this was the first spell I was able to do. This spell is mostly used to create fire. In some rare cases—"

They suddenly heard the biggest splash of all. A lava monster had arrived. Its eyes were red, and it looked like it was as angry as an infuriated ostrich.

"Hide behind a bush!" Terry told everybody. His voice was full of rage because Ms. Teach had turned this monster evil. It started screaming then left a minute later. They emerged from the bush.

"Pay attention to those sounds, because those monsters mean trouble." Matthew then asked Terry a question.

"Um...What were those ghosts you were seeing on the

battlefield? You started to say some strange things."

Terry shook his head. "If I tell you, you too will be caught up in that. Right now, let me teach you the first spell."

"Okay," Matthew agreed.

Terry nodded with excitement. "Ravysho!"

Matthew wanted to dance around and celebrate. He was about to learn his first spell, so he started to chant the words thank you. And those words came from his heart. He put his hands together and yelled the words, "Ravysho!" But nothing happened.

Terry shook his head. "When you say the word 'Ravysho', you have to say it as though it is the first sentence of a speech. As though you want the world to know you are here. Don't scream it, just say it loud and proud. And while you are saying it, loosen up. Never use it against nature and use it for good. It is okay to use it against a magical human."

Matthew nodded and for a second time he yelled the word, "Ravysho!" And he felt something magical in his throat.

* * *

Ms. Hopkins initiated the plan. She pressed an emergency button, and a sound rang right by Terry. He called her immediately. "All good, Ms. Hopkins? Are you ready for the lift?"

She responded with a scream "Yes!"

Terry looked nervous and excited. It had to be now. Victoria heard the exchange between Terry and Ms. Hopkins. She glanced out the window and saw Ms. Teach flying towards Angora with a crazy look in her eyes. And this was when Ms. Hopkins yelled the words

"Now!"

Terry's heart started pumping, while his arm was frozen. "Ishuarmandan!" he yelled in the best voice he could, and all of Angora came flying to his location, along with Sprat and all the children inside of Angora.

The students of Angora looked stunned. "That was awesome!" yelled somebody and everyone started clapping and laughing. Terry stood up on a chair and started pumping his fists in the air.

"Angora stands strong," he said. "We worked as a team. We were smart, brave, and probably a little bit lucky." Several people nodded. "Time to relax now. You've earned it."

Matthew went up to Terry who gave him a big smile. "Keep up the practice. It's just a matter of time before—"

"Ravysho!" yelled Matthew and felt disappointed when nothing happened again. He took a deep breath in and closed his eyes. He exhaled slowly. Perhaps it was best to try another time.

"Woohoo!" he heard Victoria shouting cheerfully and he ran to her and Sprat, very happy to see them both. Quickly, he updated them on his adventures on the sun. Sprat did not seem that interested and was lying down the whole time while Victoria was rubbing healing potions. Tom was also there but was not really into telling the story again (since he had already narrated it once to the Principal).

Terry breathed a sigh of relief. For now, things were quiet. He knew they had come out victorious from the recent battle and Matthew and Tom had saved the day by controlling the sun. They could enjoy themselves before training for the next battle that was sure to come.

* * *

After a good night's rest, Ms. Hopkins gathered all the students for a fun day of activities. Although she didn't tell anyone, she was also keeping her eyes open for the strongest and smartest students. Ms. Hopkins told everyone that today was sports day. "You guys will be on a team with groups A, B, C and D. And the other team will have groups F, G, H, and I. Group J is being excluded for bad behavior. It makes sense that the group with bullies is evil! They are in jail." She grunted as though she should have realized this key fact earlier. She sat down. "It starts in one hour so just prepare yourselves!"

Matthew was already on to that. He wanted to join his friends but was distracted when he saw his mom and dad. He greeted them with a big hug and an apology. But he knew he couldn't stay with them too long since he had a feeling Ms. Hopkins' sports day had something to do with helping find Ms. Teach. He instead gave them an excuse that he was going to a chicken farm.

"Oh. Our son is going to be a farmer!" exclaimed Mrs. Daniel. "Will you be able to chip in some money and get him a chicken farm?"

Mr. Daniel shook his head. "I haven't told you yet. We are practically broke. Our security cameras - the ones the burglars didn't break - have captured everything. Our house is damaged, and all our valuables stolen. We need to find a way to save what's left of our house and then sell it. We need to go back right now. Matthew, stay here where you have protection. But I can tell you there is a lightning zapping person in the non-magical community. There is something fishy going on there. And I think I know the source."

Mrs. Daniel stood still shocked and whined softly that she had a headache. Matthew didn't know what to do. He felt terrible for his parents and couldn't believe what had happened to his home. But he was hoping his father was exaggerating and that he had put away enough money in the bank to have a comfortable life. Right now, Ms. Hopkins was waving everyone over. Matthew hugged his mom again and said, "Everything will be okay, mom. I'm going to stay here a little longer, but I promise I'll be back home soon to see how you're doing. We'll figure this out."

Victoria and Tom started to line up for the race. Matthew wanted to join them but first he went to Terry to tell him the news about his family's home. He wanted to specifically mention the person who had zapping powers in Non-Magic World. Terry stood up when he heard what Matthew had to say. This was troubling indeed...

Once Matthew joined the line, he heard the end of the instructions. "The rule of this game is that you have to run to the end of this field and back. There will be about fifty of you on each team. The field is longer than the Angora field Ms. Angela has already checked. So now 3-2-1 Go Go Go!"

Matthew really thought that they were on a soccer field, but he did not know how much longer it was. He was 7th in line. The first was a boy named Karthik. Matthew wished him good luck and Karthik said that Matthew would do great. Karthik was in group A. Within a few seconds he was already crossing the first tree, going down to the second. Matthew looked at the second one in line who was a girl.

"Hi! I am Matthew! Who are you?"

But the girl just ignored him. Matthew saw the third person in line who was a boy named Tyron. "Hi, Tyron. You have a unique name."

Tyron smiled. "I heard you are a friend of my brother's. I am in second grade. You are going to have a little brother too, right?"

Matthew was surprised. "How do you know?"

Tyron shrugged. "I overheard you talking to your parents about it. You know, I know every part of Angora. I tell everyone, but they never believe me, and then they bully me."

Matthew shook his head. "That is not right of them, Tyron!"

"I don't like you," Tyron said, looking straight at Matthew. "I do not know why you were put into group E. It is still a mystery. I have already written ten letters this year to the Principal saying I wanted to be in group E. Yet you were sorted into it. I am angry. Not at you! I am angry at myself. But that doesn't mean I have to like the situation. I hope you don't mess up for the team!" he said and started to run since the second person was back. But he was slow as a turtle.

"Come on brother!" cheered Tom. Matthew was surprised that Tom had such an angry and bitter younger brother. Tyron looked sad and grumpy as he ran. He bumped his head on the first tree and apples landed on his head.

"Come on Tyron!" said Matthew, hoping these words were encouraging enough. Tyron was too angry to move though. Matthew suddenly felt a strange feeling and had the urge to whistle again. He did not want to do this in front of everybody, so he went to the back of the line, and whistled softly. A cheetah sprinted out of the woods. Matthew stared in amazement. The cheetah picked him up and they started running. The cheetah had purple spots at the bottom and red spots at the top of its body.

Even Terry was confused when he spotted the cheetah with Matthew. "What in Magic World is this?" he asked.

The other team was still in the middle of their run when the cheetah picked up Tyron. Soon though, it threw Tyron off its back. Everyone was shocked, just staring, and Matthew was the only one alert enough to catch him. Tyron looked up at Matthew gratefully. The next person was a boy named Carl. He was picked up by the cheetah who then sprinted off. And the other team was still at the end of the third lap when it was Matthew's turn. Matthew was a little grossed out when the cheetah licked him on the face, but then got over it when he was riding on its back.

"It seems like we already have a winner," announced the Principal. "So, we are moving on to the last challenge!" He told everyone to stop once Matthew had finished the ride.

"Okay," said Tyron, walking up to Matthew. "You did that, didn't you? You made the cheetah appear."

Matthew nodded. Tyron kept talking. "I am sorry. I was trying to act like someone I wasn't. But cheetahs are so cute and you're really brave. Can you believe he licked you? And I have been carried—" He stopped abruptly when he realized Matthew was still on the cheetah, who growled.

Matthew patted his back. "Say sorry to Tyron for scaring him."

Tyron gave him a smile when they heard the next announcement. "The spells competition is now between kids and adults. Let us see who will win!" Everyone got up. Each group picked on one teacher at a time. Angela trapped at least half the kids with a snap of a finger. They were stuck inside a cardboard box, including Matthew. The cheetah pounded its feet on the ground and glowered. He started chasing after Ms. Angela. And he was ten times faster than her.

"Alfa!" she said. She started to scream when the cheetah dodged the net she threw at him. "I give up! I give up!"

Terry stepped in and was not scared. With a flick of his fingers, he put the cheetah in chains. That night the whole group slept in the cardboard box. It had been a long, long day. Matthew woke up to the sound of wind howling. He crawled out of the cardboard box and saw the cheetah in pain. He came to see him.

"Um... Mr. Cheetah. I am sorry if—"

The cheetah just growled. Matthew was really in a tight situation. "I might be able to unchain you!" He looked at the sun, which was just starting to rise, and with a soft and proud voice he said, "Ravysho!" He was expecting nothing to happen, but fire appeared on his hand. Matthew suddenly understood. Fire, life. He was using this spell for good and that's why it worked. The cheetah squealed seeing the red blazing hot fire. Matthew used it to melt the chains and the cheetah was free.

"Sit! I am facing one problem after another, and helping you is going to lead to another chain of problems!" Matthew sat on the cheetah's back. "We are going to that cardboard box," he said pointing ahead. He was cut off in the middle of the sentence when the cheetah did something unimaginable. He started to fly.

"Cheetah! Stop that right now!" But then Matthew knew that the cheetah was trying to signal something to him. He started to fly over a large open area and landed in a big clump of grass. Matthew noticed that the cheetah had a scar over his right eye. That's when Matthew noticed a second cheetah. The cheetahs stood next to each other, and Matthew realized his cheetah was now with his mate. And he also realized looking at the female cheetah's big belly that she was going to have a baby.

He looked around the area. They would not be able to survive here. There was no vegetation and no other animals. Then Matthew understood why the cheetah had brought him here. He needed Matthew's help.

Matthew watched as the male cheetah's face grew sadder every second as he saw how hungry and tired his mate looked. Matthew decided that they should fly to Angora, so he sat on the male cheetah and said, "Let's go to your new home, cheetah. Have your mate come along too." The male cheetah seemed to nod his head and jumped into the air with the female cheetah right behind him.

Once Matthew and the cheetahs reached Angora, Matthew sat them down. The female cheetah lay down and her belly looked very big. The male cheetah went near her and licked her face, then looked up at Matthew. Matthew understood what he needed to do now. He started thinking about how a new cheetah cub was going to come into this world, and that made him think about his baby brother who was going to be born soon too. He cleared his throat.

"Okay, listen! To make things clear, I am not an animal expert or a scientist. I don't know how to help you with the baby, but I am going to get my friends. Stay right here!"

The cheetah growled but then made a small purring sound. He saw a gazelle jump out of a small bush. Matthew saw it but looked away and went to Victoria. It turned out the cheetah was too weak to catch the speedy gazelle, so he was still starving. Matthew woke up Victoria and Tom, and then signaled for them to stay quiet. He just whispered the words "Come with me".

Once Victoria and Tom saw the cheetahs, they were amazed. The cheetahs were huddled together, and Matthew could tell that the female was not doing well. He put a hand on her heart.

"So... Do either of you know what to do now?" Matthew asked.

Victoria nodded as though this was obvious. She got up and examined the female. "This is bad. They have not eaten in days. Plus, you're right, the female has a baby in her tummy!" She got out her first-aid kit and pulled out a small bottle and syringe to prepare a shot. She took a deep breath and injected the female cheetah who started yelping in pain. "I am so sorry. It's just that we can't let anything in your body block the baby from coming out. You need to be relaxed. Let me feel your baby," Victoria continued as she put her hand on the cheetah's belly. The cheetah started breathing loudly.

"It is in the wrong spot facing the opposite way. We have to move it upwards right now on the count of 1-2-3!" She massaged the belly and tried to get the cub to move inside. Every little inch that they got the cub to move, the cheetah would just yelp more. Soon Victoria looked up. "Okay. Now she has to do her business and get the cheetah out." The cheetah eventually started pushing and squealing. She almost woke a few people up. Victoria and Matthew would tickle her so that she would be distracted, but Tom had the most difficult job. He would put his hand on the cheetah and try to feel where the baby was.

"Take a deep breath in and out," instructed Victoria. "In and out. That is it! Good. Okay. 3-2-1 push." The baby's head soon appeared as the mom was taking deep breaths in and out.

"Deep breath, Mama! You are doing great!" Tom grunted.

Victoria kneeled right beside the mama cheetah, and soon the baby cheetahs were born. There were two of them. Everyone was really happy to see the first breaths of a new generation. Matthew was so deep in thought he forgot where he was. He knelt down, as Tom did. Their eyes widened, as they watched the two newborn cubs. And as they finally walked away, everyone had a feeling of happiness and excitement, but then they thought about their own lives and hoped

Angora's problems would be solved soon.

* * *

Mr. Daniel was on the phone with Jack. "I need a meeting now. I am making this request even though it is only 7 a.m. I need your help."

Jack sounded a little irritated when he said the next words. "Okay - come over." So, Mr. Daniel went to see Jack who was sitting in his office room. His room had the most comfortable looking desk, a daybed, a fancy treasure chest, and a closet full of the latest devices and gadgets. The house had its own park on the property and a boat resting in a small river.

"You added a boat! Really?"

Jack rolled his eyes meaning, "Yes, obviously." "Now tell me what you want. But first let me say something. I am suspicious, and when I have that feeling, I roam the world, Daniel. And you say you were in some place called Angora, but I had people check and it doesn't exist. I don't know why you lied to me."

He got up and walked towards Mr. Daniel. "I don't really need you, Daniel. You see, my niece, she has a power nobody else has, and I am going to use that to my advantage. She has the power of fire. Imagine fire shooting out of your hands."

As soon as he said that Mr. Daniel's eyes widened. "It was your niece, Melissa," he said with a trembling voice. "That's why I'm here. I came for help because someone cruel has burned down my house and stolen valuables from me. I saw a girl who could make fire appear on her hands. I can't believe that was Melissa!"

It was now Jack's turn to look surprised. "I see...So you know our secret already. Well, I can't have you reporting this to the police. It's unfortunate but now I have no choice but to keep you here. I can't have you walking out with this knowledge." And with those words, he waved for his security guards to take Mr. Daniel away. He pretended not to hear Mr. Daniel begging to be let go.

* * *

Terry was walking on the 2nd floor when he heard a bit of screeching coming from Ms. Teach's room. He opened the door and saw a chest stationed at the back corner. He opened it and to his surprise saw Ms. Ivan there. "Get me out! Ms. Teach trapped me here."

"Don't worry! We caught her a long time ago. I'm sorry we didn't rescue you sooner."

Ms. Ivan nodded and started walking with Terry. He was thinking about how he could make things normal for his students. Now that Ms. Ivan was back, and a few teachers had volunteered to take over Ms. Teach's class, they only needed one extra class to make up for the loss of Mr. Fire. Terry decided to include a new class called the Staring Beast.

Terry taught the class himself. He announced, "Everybody has to look into each other's eyes for an hour and talk. Is that clear? It will give you time to relate with someone. Now, this is very crucial to Magic World because sometimes staring into a villain's eye will give you more information on the villain."

Matthew was first assigned to sit with someone named Amy, and she was a chatterbox. "Um... How long is this class?" asked Matthew. He really wanted the class to end and get all this talking over with. Unfortunately, Amy seemed to ignore him.

"My mom used to say a train is a car that eats dragons! You find that cool, right?"

Matthew looked around for a clock. He asked urgently, "How many more minutes do we have of this amazing lesson?" She responded immediately. "55 minutes."

* * *

Ms. Hopkin's classes were getting better and better. Right now, they were learning about the battles of the Magic World.

Later that day, Matthew noticed the kids telling the Principal that they did not want the Staring Beast class again. "It is the only way for you students to really bond with each other!" the Principal kept saying.

"I don't understand," a boy yelled. "My person was really quiet. How am I supposed to be with someone like that?"

"Very well, Jason. I will partner you with someone else."

The next day, they started a new Staring Beast session. "It gives you time to reflect upon the rough times," Terry kept on saying. Nobody was encouraged by these words. Jason was sitting in the room facing Matthew. The first thing Jason did was whisper some words in Matthew's ears. "I hate this class."

Matthew sighed. This was going to be a long hour. After class, Terry had a long talk with them. "I can tell you are all extremely uncomfortable in this class, but bear with me. It is an important skill to be able to read the mind of someone using just your eyes. Let us say you two were enemies and wanted to interrogate each other, you would not even have to do that if you used the Staring Beast method."

* * *

Meanwhile, Mrs. Daniel had a Scuba Cube in her hand. She hoped this would work. "Calling Jordan for the thousandth time," she said to herself. But as usual, he didn't pick up. So, she called Matthew on the Scuba Cube hoping she could reach him. "Matthew! Pick up now." Matthew had the Scuba Cube in his hands. "Your dad is missing! He went somewhere and never returned. I don't know where he is," she said, sobbing quietly. "I will search for him on this land, but maybe you will have better luck tracking him down from Magic World."

CHAPTER NINE

THE RAINBOW OF GLEE

Jack was crouching down next to Mr. Daniel. "I can give you a little bowl of rice," said Jack. Mr. Daniel accepted it quickly.

"Jordan, the machine is nearly ready. With the power of the Scuba Cube as well as my drill, I can take control of the world and nature. As well as the people in it. Jack Company is about to expand in size."

* * *

Adam was also stuck in a room, but he was at Hornet's hideout. He missed his mom and his home. Why was Hornet holding him hostage?

As he was thinking about this, his mother Goliath was at the police station, furious that they hadn't been able to locate Hornet or her son. Suddenly, she spotted Hornet in the room, sitting on a chair, and drinking coffee calmly.

"Why did you take my son hostage, Hornet! Where is he?" she demanded to know.

Hornet shrugged. "I don't owe you any answers." He smiled. "I think you better leave, you're not safe here."

Goliath's eyes widened. "Are you threatening me in my own

156

police station?" She turned to the police officers. "Why aren't you arresting him?" she asked.

The police officers looked at her blankly. She realized they were under some kind of a trance again. "What have you done to them?" she asked Hornet in a shaky voice.

Hornet responded quietly, "Get her." Goliath started walking backwards as the police officers headed towards her. Then she started running. She looked at all the police cars. She was surrounded. There was a cliff behind the police station and no other way to escape.

"Why am I under arrest? If anybody should be under arrest it would be all of you officers who are breaking the law. You can't get away with this."

Hornet was watching her. "I'm sorry we have to do this, Goliath. But I have no choice." The police officers just laughed. And Goliath then did the craziest thing - she jumped off the cliff into a big pit below. Her heart was racing as she fell, and when she looked at the bottom of the pit more closely, she realized it had a picture of Jack's face on it. She knew he was Melissa's rich uncle, but what was an image of his face doing here? She tried to grab a branch off a tree growing on the side of the cliff as she was falling, but she missed, and it was as though she was falling onto his face. And when she was about to crash into his nose, she noticed that written across his forehead were the words "Trip to Antarctica!" She landed with a thump and found herself inside an electronic box and was zoomed into Antarctica. She was dropped into a big drilling rig at least 2,000 feet tall. She landed there stunned when the entire drilling rig started to move.

* * *

Matthew went to Victoria and Tom and told them that his dad had gone missing. He felt like a robot, stunned, as he shared his mom's feeling that there may be clues to where his dad was on Magic World. "Mom thinks there's a connection between the two worlds," said Matthew, looking miserable.

"This time we need more people to help," said both Victoria and Tom, more or less at the same time.

"Should we ask Terry for help?" asked Matthew.

Victoria shook her head. "No! At this point anyone here could be working with Ms. Teach, including Terry. I think he's a good person, but we don't know for sure..."

"Oh," remarked Matthew, embarrassed that he hadn't thought about that.

"I think we can trust our friends," continued Victoria. "Let's ask a few people who we think would be up for this challenge and who would keep our activities a secret."

Tom first asked Tyron and Matthew asked Jason. They both said yes. Tom also asked someone named Michael and Victoria approached a girl named Isabelle.

"Okay!" said Victoria. "I don't think the clues are within the walls of Angora. We need to organize and sneak outside Angora to figure out where Matthew's dad is." The group arranged to sneak out after dinner. As they stepped outside school, an alarm started to ring.

"Where are you going?" yelled Terry, teleporting to the

entrance of the school. He caught Matthew's eye. "I need everyone to get back inside. Now!" As the students ignored him, Terry used his wand to summon security. A giant robot arrived and at the bottom of its screen were printed the words, "Bring Back The Naughty Kids!" It started using giant tweezers to try to pick up everyone.

"I never knew the first step would be so hard!" yelled Victoria as she was plucked by the robot and was hanging upside down. It started shooting ice cubes at everyone.

"Let's get away!" shouted Matthew. But the Principal teleported the robot right behind them. Big balls came swerving at them now and slowed down their pace. Suddenly they heard something rustling in the bushes. Only Matthew, Victoria, and Tom knew what it was. The cheetah and his family emerged from a nearby bush and flew to the head of the robot. It bit off its ears and nose. Matthew watched the cubs who were taking the bottom half of the robot apart. It started shooting lasers at the cheetah, but the female bit off his legs. The robot started to fall and fall until it was no more.

"No! Little cheetah pests. I will teleport myself right next to the children!" But before Terry could use his wand, one of the cheetah cubs jumped into the air and grabbed his wand. He started chewing on it and ran happily back to join his family.

Matthew and the others kept running while Terry looked at them angrily. "Sorry Principal Terry! We'll be back soon!" he yelled.

* * *

Back in Ireland, Jack was sitting in his office watching his guards type a bit of programming. "Ah! Guards, our program is almost done.

Soon our secret lab will be ready." Jack had a private portal to the drilling rig in his own house. He jumped in but landed headfirst on a glacier in Antarctica.

"Hey, wasn't I supposed to land on the drill rig?" Suddenly, right behind him he saw something unbelievable. "Easy lava monster, easy does it." The orange blaze of fire was steaming hot and melting Antarctica. The monster started shooting fire at Jack who quickly ran away.

* * *

Mr. Fire the Second was sitting on a tree branch meditating, "Om! Om! Om!" The wind started blowing harder and more distracted thoughts came into Fire the Second's mind. He saw a picture of the black cloaked man shaking his brother's body. He decided to lie down to rest when he heard a noise.

"Hop two three four!" yelled Victoria and Mr. Fire the Second raised his head, recognizing the voice. He obviously remembered Victoria, Tom, and Matthew but he was too tired to move from his hiding spot. When they came and stood below his tree he said, "You won! Bring me back to the Principal if you want and do your business!"

They were all surprised when they looked up and spotted Mr. Fire the Second. Tom was the first one to respond. "We are on a different quest, Mr. Fire. We were not asked to bring you to Angora!"

Mr. Fire the Second nodded and said sarcastically, "Which is why you brought the cheetah! And it has a family. I give up. I do."

Victoria told the others it was probably best to walk away from Mr. Fire the Second as the cheetah cubs growled. When they were a few minutes away, Mr. Fire decided to follow the kids. They walked for an hour and Matthew slowed down at a tree. He was very tired and yawned. Everyone around him yawned too. "Let's stay here for the night," said Matthew. "The cheetahs will watch over us."

They made themselves as comfortable as possible and went to sleep. The next morning, Matthew decided they needed a better plan since they had no idea where they were going and what they were looking for. Plus, they needed to be faster. He looked around at the group and made a decision. "Let's do this faster. One person goes on one of the baby cheetah's backs, and another person goes on the other baby cheetah. Two of us can travel on the female cheetah and the remaining three on the male."

Matthew, Tom, and Victoria went on the male, while Tyron and Jason went on the female. Michael and Isabelle were each on the baby cheetahs. They heard a twig snap and looked back and thought they saw someone. "Is that Mr. Fire?" asked Victoria, looking carefully. "Why is he following us and acting so strange?"

Tom frowned. "That is not Mr. Fire! Ms. Hopkins confirmed my suspicion back in Angora. That is definitely Mr. Fire the Second. He must be sad, and he must now think that we do not know his brother is dead. And—"

He was cut off when the cheetahs started to fly. "Whoa, easy cheetah." Those who were flying for the first time were both amazed and terrified. The cheetahs were swirling all across the sky and Tom thought he was going to smash into an oak tree when they dipped down. They started zigzagging around the light blue sky shining bright and standing out to the world. After an hour they landed on the ground, and it took them a few minutes to adjust to their surroundings. Leaves started falling from the trees around them. They looked around and spotted many stones on the ground.

Jason stretched out and rested his foot on one of the stones. A second later there was a boom and bang. The stones started to explode. "What's happening?" he screamed. A heavy breeze started to rise, and it hit lots of trees, a few of which started to topple over. As more trees fell, the nature around them started to weaken.

"This is bad," yelled Victoria.

"Yeah, I really have not noticed that!" screamed back Tom sarcastically.

Suddenly a huge demon arrived. She had green eyes, a yellow tail, black hair, and yellow teeth. "Where is Hopkins! She has broken her oath to protect the Haspura stone," snarled the big monster. All the rocks started to rise and shatter. "But let me first destroy anyone in my path!" She cast a spell at them, and sharp rocks appeared in the air pointing at the students.

Ms. Hopkins could feel the children were in danger and teleported right to the scene. "You must not harm them!" she yelled, but she was powerless with the cursed necklace. "They did not know they were disturbing the Haspura rock."

The demon created an earthquake and the ground rumbled. Ms. Hopkins jumped up and teleported a few steps away. But they shifted the tremors of the earthquake.

"Oh bummer," shrieked Ms. Hopkins. Rocks started falling from cliffs, almost hitting everyone. "Move out!" she screamed from the back, but with all the thumping rocks, they could not hear her.

"You cannot stop me," exclaimed the demon. The cheetah and his family were behind Matthew and were super scared. She spun around casting spells all around herself.

"Get back on, this time, pick up Ms. Hopkins and retreat!" commanded Matthew. The students quickly scrambled around and got back to their positions on the cheetahs. Ms. Hopkins quickly jumped on with Jason and Tyron.

She looked around in amazement as the demon started shouting insults, staring up at them. "That was too easy!" yelled Victoria but Ms. Hopkins shook her head.

"We are still in battle!" she said. "Right now, she might be persuading the Weather Lord to help bring us down. We better land somewhere before that happens." But her words came too late. Lightning started to strike, and a new thunderstorm was coming. "We gave humans a privilege! Now it is broken!" a voice growled.

Streaks of fire were shooting all over. "I can't teleport you all to Angora because I do not know where we are in the sky." Winds were hitting the male cheetah with force. "However risky it is, we have to land now!" yelled Ms. Hopkins.

Matthew tapped the cheetah's back and said, "Land," hoping that simple word would be understood by the cheetah. The cheetah started to crash land. But lightning was still striking all around him.

"Come on, cheetah!" encouraged Tom. So, the cheetah did the most reasonable thing, he crashed into a bush, and the other cheetahs followed him.

* * *

The lava monsters were melting the glaciers in Antarctica.

"Well, this drilling rig was no use!" said one of the guards. But Jack shook his head. "The drilling rig will help us pave Antarctica once the glaciers melt. For now, we just can't crash into the lava monsters."

The guards nodded. Then Jack's smartest guard came forward. He was a scientist that had green eyes, white hair, and black clothing that had the words **J is For Jack** embroidered on it.

"I have a theory that is probably fifty percent true. Remember when we had a complete blackout? I had special telescopes in place focused on the sun. I've reviewed the data and it showed that the sun's temperature decreased in those five minutes. My theory is that those lava monsters were able to adapt to the low temperature drop on the sun and are now suited to the environment here in Antarctica."

Jack scratched his head thoughtfully. "You really think those lava monsters came down from the sun?"

The scientist nodded. "But there's more. The sun cannot drop its temperature suddenly without something major happening. And my telescopes didn't pick up anything strange. But when I looked carefully at the images during the blackout - although it was dark - you might call me crazy, but I think I saw a second sun. This second sun seemed to be revolving around the moon. I think something happened on the second sun which caused a blackout everywhere in the universe. I cannot put everything together, but what I am trying to say is that these lava monsters came down not from our sun but an unexplored second sun."

He paused and looked up. Jack raised his eyebrows and was looking at him with a mix of amazement and disbelief.

* * *

Melissa, John, Emily, and Joanne were in Ireland at Jack's house while he was away, guarding Mr. Daniel who was locked in a room.

"Please! I don't want to cause trouble, but Jack is hiding me because he is planning something big that can hurt a lot of people," said Mr. Daniel.

Emily shook her head. "Melissa has been through a lot. We don't want to hear this - don't exhaust her." Mr. Daniel put his head in his hands and groaned softly. "Your friend Melissa destroyed my house and now seems keen to destroy me too." He looked like he would be trapped there indefinitely.

* * *

Matthew was stuck in a cranberry bush. At least there was something to eat. Everyone was really thirsty though, so food did not help. Ms. Hopkins plucked a few cranberries and she chewed on them with a thoughtful expression on her face.

They emerged from the bush, but the male cheetah had a thorn in his paw. "Um... Ms. Hopkins, please help because I am not good at helping animals in pain," said Tom. Ms. Hopkins nodded and within a few seconds she plucked out the thorn.

165

"I have taught veterinary care. Victoria knows," commented Ms. Hopkins. Matthew looked down at his shoes. There were purple cranberries stuck to it, so he threw them back into the bush. Then they got back on the cheetahs, and this time they travelled on land.

They were too far to hear the Weather Lord who was sitting on a throne, incredibly angry. "I trusted myself to protect the stone!" he yelled angrily and hit himself. The green monster was right next to him.

"The promise has been broken and has backfired on us. We will no longer have the strength we once did. Now we have one more thing to worry about. Ms. Hopkins, get ready to face your doom!"

Ms. Hopkins meanwhile was sitting with Tyron and Jason on their cheetah. "I should have told you about the promise." She shook her fists angrily. "When I was about five years old, I wandered away from my family while on a hike, slipped and landed on a rock. That was the rock of Haspura. There was an explosion, similar to what happened today, and the monster was furious because that stone is what gave her much of her power. But she knew I was just an innocent kid, so she let me go, and said in return I had to use my powers to guard the rock. So, I swore to the Lords that I would protect the rock, but I failed. Now I will be chased by the Lords forever, until I die."

Jason gulped. "I'm so sorry for causing trouble. I have a question... Have I automatically been sworn to protect the rock from now on, because I was the one who touched it?"

Ms. Hopkins nodded, and Jason was upset with himself.

"I know we are all very emotional now. But we have to keep

going," said Tyron. They reached a river, and everyone was so relieved that they jumped into the water. The water tasted so fresh.

"I'll take 100 water bottles for the trip," said Ms. Hopkins as she followed up with the words, "Aliffel 100!" 100 bottles showered down with lids. Ms. Hopkins filled them all with water, put the caps on and stored the bottles in a magic box.

"Let's take a boat and travel on the river for a little while," suggested Victoria. They spotted an old boat off to the side, tied to a tree on the riverbank. The cheetahs looked a little nervous and were huddled together on the boat. Matthew patted their heads to comfort them.

"Let's see where the current takes us," he said, as the boat started to float down the river.

* * *

Once Ms. Hopkins and the others found an island to stop at, they came down from the boat. "Much better!" she said. "Anyway, we really have to make a plan to search for Mr. Daniel. We can't randomly go everywhere. We need a good, solid, plan. And—"

She was interrupted by the male cheetah licking her. "Ew," squealed Ms. Hopkins as she went farther away from the cheetah.

Isabelle raised her hand. "I think that we should go to the Cracks of Jin. I know where it is, follow me. I don't know why I didn't think of it before. I read about it in a book recently. It will show us where your father is Matthew, and also how he disappeared and everything else! Follow me."

Ms. Hopkins eyed Isabelle with interest. This young girl

seemed to know a lot. She had barely spoken at school, yet here she was acting like a leader. Why did she get the feeling that she was hiding something though? Ms. Hopkin decided to keep a close eye on her as the group went back to the boat. They sailed and sailed, with Isabelle at the steering wheel. Matthew was feeling optimistic that they would finally get some answers about his father.

"Okay! Where are the Cracks of Jin?" asked Tom enthusiastically.

"We set off for sea and into the Rainbow of Glee, then we find the armor of Jin, and finally go through the last glass shard!" exclaimed Isabelle.

Ms. Hopkins looked at her. "How do you know this is the way there?" she asked. "Who told you?"

Isabell shrugged, confused. "I don't remember. I think a book called *A Guide to the Cracks of Jin.*"

Ms. Hopkins did not know this book, but Victoria broke up the conversation and said that they should just trust her. "Okay! We first set off to the Rainbow of Glee. Let's go!"

"We must sail to the Rainbow of Glee," repeated Matthew. Michael frowned. "I thought it was a myth."

Jason then corrected him. "Actually, there is such a thing. My mother told me once about my great-great-great grandma getting stuck in the Rainbow of Glee, and she never came out. Matthew's dad might be stuck there too."

They went back to steering the boat. Then Matthew got a call from Jack on his Scuba Cube. "The person most likely to become

President of Non-Magic World is calling me. Should I answer?"

Tom was too excited to speak and was hoping to listen to the conversation, but Matthew told him it was private. He picked up the phone and listened. "Hello, Matthew! I was checking to see if you found your dad yet. Poor man he is, poor man!" said Jack.

Matthew was sad that he didn't have an update. He would be letting everyone down, most importantly his dad, if he did not find him soon.

"How did you know he was missing?" asked Matthew, genuinely surprised.

Jack laughed. "I know everything! You forget he works for me. Also, your mom called to ask for my help. How is Angora by the way?"

Matthew was confused on how Jack knew where he was. He was sure his mom would never have shared that information. He made an excuse and said that he was in Ireland.

"Well, I am in Antarctica, working on a drill rig. Anyway, good luck to you. I hope you find him. Bye!"

When Jack hung up, he scrolled through the Scuba Cube. "Give me Matthew's coordinates. I need his location when he picked up my call." A robotic voice answered. "Unidentified, Unidentified, Unidentified!" Then there was a bar graph with blazing colors. "Magic," chanted the robot.

* * *

As the yellow ball of fire was burning down on Matthew's head, he got up and told everyone about the call.

"I don't know if we're on the right track, Matthew," complained Tom. "The Rainbow of Glee, find the armory of Jin, the last glass shard. It makes sense but doesn't at the same time."

Victoria nodded. "It is too confusing! I am also questioning if this is the correct way to go about finding your father."

Matthew nodded. "I agree. We can't be blindly doing something and expecting an answer in return. But as we've discussed, we need a good plan."

The cheetahs were up from their nap and licked everyone. "Again, why are we going to listen to Isabelle based on a book she supposedly read?" questioned Tom, but Victoria punched him lightly on the shoulder. "I trust Isabelle, and it's not her fault if we get lost. She is smart and won't let it happen! I am sure of that."

Tom clenched his teeth. "If we end up being stuck somewhere or are in danger, I'm going to make sure Isabelle pays for it."

Matthew went to Ms. Hopkins to be comforted. "Please tell me you think this journey is a good idea."

Ms. Hopkins smacked her lips. "For every action you take, there will be a good effect and a bad effect. You must know who you want to trust, and you must think of every possibility of what may happen. I trust you, Matthew. I have faith in you, even though you are not from a magical family. But you need to decide who you trust, and why. This is not just an easy task. The Principal talks a lot about chess, with lots of strategies and possibilities, because he has already been wrong about trusting someone he should not have. So, keep in mind that who you choose to trust can have a serious impact on all of us." She walked away, knowing Matthew had a lot to think about.

An hour later, Matthew stood next to Isabelle. "Okay. I want to trust you Isabelle, but I feel like you're hiding something. Are you on our side?"

Isabelle looked up and nodded her head.

He walked away still unsure as Isabelle kept steering the boat. "I know what I'm doing!" she whispered to herself.

Michael and Tyron were playing with the cheetah. Matthew went up to them. "I want you both to know that I appreciate the risks you've taken to be with me."

Michael gave him a smile. "Whether you have known someone for years or met recently, you have to offer support and believe the best in each other. That's what friends are for!"

Matthew gave a sigh of relief.

* * *

Mr. Daniel was still in chains with Melissa on guard. He could hear her talking to her friends outside.

"My father is alive! I can't believe it. My Uncle Jack is sure of it." She looked at Emily, Joanne, and John for their reactions. Joanne gasped. "That's amazing! I'm so happy for you." The others nodded, smiling.

"Mr. Daniel, I'm feeling very generous," said Melissa. "If you do something for me, I can get you out of this room." Mr. Daniel was not feeling very optimistic about this, but he said okay.

"Great! I need you to convince my grandmother to lend us a

yacht," said Melissa.

Mr. Daniel looked startled. "Did you just say a yacht? Why on Earth would a kid like you want a yacht. And why do you need me to get it for you?"

Melissa scoffed. "Answer to the first question is, none of your business. To answer the second question, my grandmother Helen appreciates you for building the Scuba Cube, plus you're an adult. There is a better chance that she will agree to your request rather than mine. So...Are you going to do it?"

Mr. Daniel took a deep breath in and out, and declared, "Fine, it is certainly better than being stuck in here."

* * *

Ms. Hopkins was sitting on the boat. Victoria walked over to her, and she looked up. "The sky is like the sea today," whispered Mrs. Hopkins. Then she looked down at her necklace, which always reminded her of the sea, and sadly remembered that there was something wrong with it as it would not come off. "Victoria, why do you look so down?"

Victoria blinked away tears. "I'm just sad. When my father passed, I felt that life as we knew it would be over. My mother was not even magical. She was searching hard for a job. I did not know what to do, until I met you. You always drop off new kids, and the Principal gives you that job because he is counting on you to make us feel comfortable. But thinking about how Matthew's father is missing makes me miss my dad, too."

Ms. Hopkins looked at Victoria sympathetically and got up

to give her a hug.

On the other side of the boat, Matthew was talking to Tom. "I do not think we should be on this boat anymore," he said looking a bit seasick. "No kidding," replied Tom as they started walking to the back of the boat to Ms. Hopkins and Victoria. The boat suddenly started shaking.

"Um... Does everyone know how to swim because I don't," confessed Tom.

Matthew let out a long breath. "Swimming in open water is hard. I can barely do it."

Victoria looked out at the water. "What's going on? It seems like we're heading towards a storm."

Jason, Tyron, Michael, and Isabelle all came over as the sky around them got dark. "We need to get out of here. There is a hurricane heading our way," Isabelle said.

Ms. Hopkins nodded. "Plus, no one is steering the boat!" They started to sink underwater as the biggest waves came crashing down. "Everyone jump off!" she yelled. "Don't worry if you're not comfortable swimming. I'm going to cast a spell to keep us all invisibly connected and floating."

Isabelle was pointing right once they jumped into the water. In a muffled tone Ms. Hopkins said, "That is the wrong way. You're pointing us towards the hurricane." But as Isabelle swam to her right, Victoria followed her.

"Oh man," said Jason. He was finding it hard to stay afloat and was grateful that Ms. Hopkins who keeping an eye on him.

Tyron panicked when he noticed that the cheetah cubs were drowning. The male cheetah and his mate were bobbing their heads in and out of the water, but they were struggling.

Michael squinted his eyes at Tom. "You told me you saved them once, save them again." Tom shook his head, unsure of what to do, but Jason dunked Tom underwater and was right behind him as Tom grabbed the two cubs around their bellies.

"Come on," begged Tyron, waiting for Tom to resurface. Tom muttered the words, "Juio!" in a quiet tone. He and the cheetah cubs sprouted up from the water along with Jason and landed on Tyron.

Matthew was fighting off the big waves crashing down on him. He was bound to get crushed in the next round. He had to jump over all the waves, and on top of that, the sky had lightning shooting down.

"Where do we go now? We've lost them," complained Tyron. "We have to find Victoria, Isabelle and Ms. Hopkins."

Bigger waves were emerging now. Tom looked to Michael for comfort. He knew he was always calm in an emergency. "Do you have any ideas?" asked Tom.

Michael nodded. "Usio," he yelled. Suddenly, he had two large suction cups on his hands. He jumped up as a big wave hit but was swatted back down by a big tentacle. Tyron screamed.

* * *

Melissa's mom, Alissa, was at her mother's house. It was huge, with big stone statues of tigers, lions, zebras, and snakes on top of the

174

house. All statues were carved into the rooftop. Alissa was identical to Melissa, with the same golden hair. The only difference was that she was taller. When she walked in, she saw the butler and nine other staff members standing in a corner, plus a fancy chair, and a teapot, made of marble. As she went up the marble staircase, she noticed sparkling crystals that looked like diamonds in the ceiling. She reached the top of the stairs and saw golden walls in a majestic room. And, of course, on the first golden chair was Alissa's mother. She had light skin and white hair, blue eyes, and a red shirt like the color of roses.

"I knew you would need my help at one point," said the old woman softly.

* * *

Michael stood up tall on his tippy toes and started using his suction cups again. The storm was getting worse right now, and he didn't know what creature that tentacle belonged to. Matthew grabbed one of the cheetahs as Michael put his hands in the water again. Matthew got on top of one of the cheetah cubs saying, "Let's hope this works."

"Everyone, get on a cheetah!" yelled Matthew, but of course they were separated from the other cheetahs by then. The waves were growing larger and larger. "It is not going to work, Matthew. No one can withstand these waves," shouted Michael.

Matthew shook his head. "We can't give up. Heat can evaporate water. Maybe we can use a spell to stop the waves."

Tom yelled in a panicked voice. "We cannot produce that

much fire. It is too much."

"Yes, you can," said a familiar voice behind them. They turned to see Mr. Fire the Second. "Asay Raga," he yelled, his voice sounding different. He sounded happier now, maybe because he found a purpose in helping someone in need. And as more fire came swirling around, it made everything brighter. The waves started to subside.

"Someone, get the cheetahs," shouted Matthew. Michael swam and found all the cheetahs who were whimpering. Michael got on one of the cheetahs with Tyron. The rest managed to get on cheetahs too.

"Let's go!" he yelled, but Matthew held up his hand. "Wait, lightning is shooting from the sky. We can't get past that. I do not know what to do."

But Mr. Fire jumped in. "Trust me kiddo, sometimes a grown-up has something up his sleeve a kid does not expect." Matthew did not know if that was a quote, or just a random thing Mr. Fire came up with. But in any case, he listened to Mr. Fire.

"Okay. This won't hurt your cheetahs. It will just make them go faster." He put his two hands on the first cheetah. "Go." As he said those words, the first cheetah started zooming like a rocket ship. One by one the cheetahs took off.

Victoria, meanwhile, was in the water trying to grab Isabelle's arms. "It is not going to work! We need to go the other way," she screamed, but Isabelle ignored her.

"We need to go to the Rainbow of Glee," she shouted back.

"This is the only way!"

Ms. Hopkins was following them. "Everyone else has gone away from the hurricane. We have to go," she pleaded. But Isabelle just kept going. Victoria could not reach Isabelle's legs to stop her, even Ms. Hopkins couldn't.

"I will save everyone, Victoria! Trust me!" And suddenly, leaving her with those words, Isabelle seemed to jump into a giant wave which parted to reveal a small island, in front of which was a colorful, round shaped object.

"A portal," whispered Ms. Hopkins, in a tone that sounded more happy than angry. "Victoria, this is good, we should go right now."

It seemed like the ocean floor was starting to rumble and Ms. Hopkins knew what she had to do. "Okay, I am jumping in," she yelled as she dived into the portal. Victoria was frozen, staring at where Ms. Hopkins had disappeared when she noticed the cheetahs had landed on the island on the other side.

"Looks like this is the right way after all," Victoria thought gratefully.

On the island, where the cheetahs and their passengers had safely landed, Jason was looking worried. "They're coming after me," he whispered softly. He was sure that the demon was trying to track him down and punish him for upsetting the Haspura rock. "I think I can go with Mr. Fire the Second to Angora. Even though we do not know the exact location, he knows the general area. Wait, do you know the new location of Angora?"

Mr. Fire shook his head, "But I think I might know a location close to it." Jason scratched his forehead. "How do you know what's close to Angora?" he asked.

"Because I have seen these cheetahs flying near there," replied Mr. Fire. "They have a remarkable ability to track down Angora," he stated. "Let's take them with us." Jason glanced at Matthew for his permission. He nodded his head. And with that, Jason and all four cheetahs teleported with Mr. Fire.

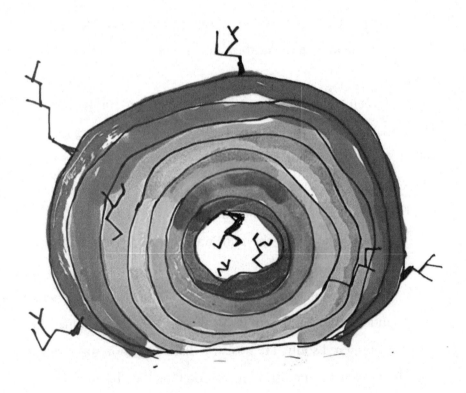

Once the others were organized on the island, they looked at each other to see who would enter the portal first. Victoria took the lead. She closed her eyes, hoping that she would be okay, trying to think of the best times in her life. She put her hands on her ears, probably because she wanted to block out the noise, and dove into the portal. Second was Tom, then Tyron, then Michael. The last one was Matthew. He knew he did not have time to wait, because the island was about to get destroyed, so he quickly smashed into the portal. It felt like he was zooming through time and space, as though he was in a wormhole. Once he popped out, he was in a different land. There were hundreds of golden trees. Matthew wanted to climb up them but controlled himself.

"Wow," said Tyron, taking it all in. Isabelle was staring too. "The Rainbow of Glee," she gasped. She jumped up and down like a little kid on Christmas morning about to open her presents. Victoria and Tom were looking at a big tree. It had especially big golden branches that dropped to the ground.

"I want to know where my dad is," said Matthew, bringing back focus to their journey.

"We need to find the armor of Jin the Yard," said Isabelle, nodding her head at Matthew. They started to walk.

Ms. Hopkins was at the back of the group. "I am not sure!" she kept on saying. "Are we trusting the right person?" She walked up to Isabelle. "Okay, do you know anything about all the risks you are taking? And how many lives are at stake? This is not the right way to do this."

Isabelle looked coldly at Ms. Hopkins. Her eyebrows were raised, indicating that she didn't like how this conversation was going.

"Why don't you trust me? I just do not understand!" She started to skip away. Isabelle turned around and saw Ms. Hopkins struggling to walk. "Come on! Move quicker," she yelled. Ms. Hopkins gritted her teeth and started to run but was unable to maintain her speed. The cursed necklace was dragging her down. She made up an excuse and said her leg was injured. Ms. Hopkins tried to use a spell against the necklace, but it was no use. It was as though Ms. Teach was controlling it.

Ms. Hopkins made her way to Matthew. "What exactly did Ms. Teach say, when you were fighting her," she asked.

"I already told everyone what I know. Wait! She did mention my friend's name at some point which I thought was strange. She said Adam – he's my best friend in Non-Magic World - and she also mentioned a man named Hornet? Apparently, he has captured my friend Adam. I really hope they find him soon."

Ms. Hopkins looked at him seriously. "I need to get back to Angora now! I need to tell Terry about Hornet right away." She paused for a second and asked, "Matthew, why don't you come back with me. I know you're hoping to find your father, but I'm not sure there are any answers here. And I don't completely trust Isabelle."

Matthew shook his head. "I need to be here. I can feel it. And I can't abandon my friends. They came here to help me."

Ms. Hopkins nodded understandingly. "Be safe," she said. "I'll be keeping an eye on you."

Before Matthew could ask her what she meant by that, Ms. Hopkins quickly teleported away.

"Well, I think we lost the only grown-up who can help us," Matthew whispered to himself.

He joined the rest of the group. "We have to press forward. We have no other choice," exclaimed Isabelle and Tom nodded. She pointed to a clearing near a few trees. "We can stay here for the night."

Everyone was exhausted and lay down to rest. In the middle of the night, Isabelle got up. She looked around to ensure nobody was looking. Then, she smiled and looked at a tree. Inside the tree was the reflection of Hornet. "Father! They will come here, I know it. Angora can be yours, all of it. I know the new location."

Hornet's image nodded but said, "I think we should go with plan B. Do not draw any more suspicion and make sure Ms. Hopkins comes back. You have to earn her trust."

A few hours later the group woke up. Isabelle stared at them like a wasp about to sting a human. Then she forced herself to smile. "Well, come on, let's go!"

Everyone was tired and hungry. Isabelle seemed to know where to go so they followed her.

"Find the armor of Jin the Yard? Who is that? And go through the last glass shard? I do not understand," said Victoria. Matthew nodded, "But we have to try. I just know that."

They started to climb up the golden trees and got a good view. "Nothing for miles! Just a big heap of junk," uttered Michael.

"I found Jin the Yard." Isabelle pointed to a big junk yard that Michael had spotted earlier.

Matthew nodded. "Good. Now bring us to the armor."

Tom looked at them as though they might have been heading the wrong way. The whole junkyard was filled with bones piling up and cobwebs all around. And the weird thing was that it looked like the face of a monster.

"I wonder why this is called Jin the Yard," said Michael.

"I don't know what to do with this face staring at me!" said Tom super concerned. Everyone turned to where Tom was looking. There was an enormous skull sitting there. "That's Jin! Jin the Yard, and I am pretty sure that's his armor!"

Tyron walked toward the head, but Tom pushed him away. "Do not use your staring powers to see if his spirit is alive, Tyron. It is too dangerous."

But Tyron ignored his brother and kept on walking. Victoria looked at him urgently and said with panic in her voice, "He is going to get swallowed." Tom did not know what to do, so he said, "Oga Booga!"

They heard a sudden roar and started to run. Matthew's legs were killing him, and that was when he heard a cracking sound. Tyron was in the skull's mouth. And then he disappeared.

Tom fell to the ground and cried out loud. He was so angry and upset that he couldn't stop his brother from walking into the skull. He was devastated. But then Victoria started examining the skull from far away and said, "He is lost in time. This is the skull of Karkatu. Your brother is not dead, Tom. He is stuck in a portal and just trapped in time. We can't all risk going after him – so I suggest we split up. One group searches for Tyron and one searches for Matthew's father."

Everyone in the group was still shocked at what had happened. Victoria continued, "Tom and I can search for Tyron, and Matthew, Michael and Isabelle can search for clues to Mr. Daniel's whereabouts."

Tom was howling like crazy. "My brother! He can't be dead! I need to find him."

Suddenly the skull growled. Victoria shook her head, "This is bad. The skull has been disturbed. Tom and I have to jump into the skull. Good luck to you guys finding Mr. Daniel." They hugged each other and with that she and Tom jumped into the skull.

"We have to run. This is the armor of Jin the Yard! You might not understand but we have to get away from this horrible beast. We have to go straight!" Michael grabbed Matthew's hand and pulled him along. Matthew was exhausted and knew he wouldn't be able to outrun even a tortoise.

"Go, Michael! I will find a way out! Go!" yelled Matthew as Michael finally started running. Matthew put his hands together and looked at the skull. "I do believe there is good in you, skull. I do not know who you are or what you are but—"

Okay, maybe this plan did not work because this skull was not nature. This gave Matthew an idea. "Calling all nature!" He whistled. "Come to the only Nature Spirit on land." But then the skull grew bigger and bigger, hands were rising from its head. It started turning gold and soon he was a golden tree. Matthew stood rooted to the spot until one of the branches hit him.

* * *

Terry started banging his head on the refrigerator door once he heard Ms. Hopkins' news about Hornet. "I am not battling my friend."

Ms. Hopkins snorted before saying, "This is not only about your friend. Matthew also has a friend who is being held captive. And who knows how many others he might have captured."

Terry pounded his fists on the table. "I should have known! You do not understand how much I thought about the return of Hornet. For ten years do you think I was doing nothing? That's far from the truth."

* * *

Jack was sitting in the drilling rig when Goliath came up with a glue gun in her hand. She had found it lying on the drill.

"You're Jack, aren't you?" asked Goliath. She aimed the glue gun at him. "I know you are Melissa's uncle. But how did I get here? I was in Ireland one minute and the next minute I'm falling over a cliff into some kind of portal. Where am I?"

That was when a lady emerged onto the drill. She was wearing pink clothing from top to bottom and had pink nail polish on her fingers. She also had big hoop earrings with Australian opals. A camera hung around her neck.

She was talking to someone on her phone. "Let's rendezvous back here at exactly 3:00 p.m.," the mysterious woman said in a confident voice. "Bye."

Jack stared at her. "Who are you?" he asked, his voice full of wonder.

"Now, I think it would be a more reasonable question to ask about the woman who is going to shoot you with a glue gun. Come on, let us have a chat."

Goliath stared at the lady. "Aren't you going to introduce yourself first? You're clearly a stranger to everyone."

The mysterious lady nodded. "I am a stranger here, but not back home. Everyone knows me there. I am Tanu," she said.

Goliath did not know whether to shake hands with her or say something mean so she went with her instincts. "I really do not like you," she said.

Tanu nodded. "Yes. I can understand. Maybe you should think of it in a different way. Let us say that I am angry at you because you ruined my pink clothing and earrings. I would take a deep breath in and out and then move on. It always works. Now, I have a few questions for both of you."

Goliath narrowed her eyes at her. She had ruined her plans to get Jack to send her back home and was now being questioned? She had to be careful around this woman.

* * *

Michael and Isabelle were a few minutes away from Matthew when they stopped running. "We are down to only two people on this adventure. I don't think that's smart. We have to turn back and get Matthew," said Isabelle. Michael agreed so they started sprinting back towards the skull. Once they saw the gigantic golden tree, they started approaching it carefully, but the tree ignored their attempt to be friendly and pulled them up.

Matthew glared at the two of them. "Why did you come back here? Just to get caught?"

"We thought it would be better to stick together. But we are so dead...," said Michael. They were trying to fall from the tree but couldn't. They were stuck.

"I think the tree wants to prove that there is life here," said Matthew thoughtfully.

Michael started arguing with him. "You think you know everything. Well, we're in a fine mess and I don't think you have any clue of what to do." One of the branches scratched Michael's neck lightly and he started screeching, "It is evil! I see his look, pure evil!" He was soon flung from the tree and hit the ground hard. Isabelle stared in disbelief then took a knife out of her pocket but the golden branch from the tree flung itself at her from the side. It hit her on the nose.

Matthew did not want to hurt the tree, but he also did not want to get hurt himself. "Down," he commanded the tree in a confident voice and the tree put him down. Michael stared at him and said in amazement, "Oh! Why didn't you tell me that was all we needed to do?"

Matthew blinked and said in an annoyed tone, "You said I did not know anything." He then looked at Isabelle. "And you brought out a knife. Apologize to the tree right now."

Isabelle gave Matthew a look of disbelief. "We were stuck on a tree," she said. "And you want me to apologize to it? That's not my style." She started to cut down the tree branch by branch. The tree fought back and cut her, wounding her eye.

Isabelle screamed in pain. "You are right, Matthew. It is too powerful. I don't want to lose an eye for this." As they were leaving, Isabelle looked at the tree and whispered in a soft tone, "Escavor." Soon the tree started shriveling millimeter by millimeter.

* * *

Meanwhile, inside the skull, Tom shook his fists. He and Victoria were next to each other. "I need to see my brother now!" yelled Tom desperately. They were in a sandy area.

"We are in the past," said Victoria looking around. "I recognize it. This is the Magic Beach in the year 10,000. It was created by an explosion of the big tides. We've been transported back in time."

Tom remarked, "Tyron was flashed here. I am not giving up until I find him. Are you with me?"

Victoria nodded sincerely. "We have to find your brother. I just hope he was not flashed into the sand. It's a sinkhole. That is where we need to first search for Tyron."

Tom shivered. It was obvious he was scared. Back on the other side of the skull/tree, Matthew was observing Isabelle's eyes. They were purple and black on the sides. Sunlight was streaming through the trees and leaves started falling on her face.

Soon, Isabelle complained to Matthew that she was tired. He felt bad knowing she was hurt, even if he felt there was something odd and dangerous about her. They found a quiet area under some trees to rest.

* * *

Tanu was sitting next to both Goliath and Jack. "As a journalist, I need to ask some questions. Goliath, what would you do if you were a celebrity? I have seen you onscreen you know. You are head of the police force in Ireland, aren't you?"

Goliath gazed at her steadily. "Yes, and a teacher too. I was born to be a leader and win."

Tanu nodded. "If that is your opinion, I support it. I was not only born to be a winner now, I was born a winner in my past life."

Jack spoke up sounding confused. "Yeah, well, as an actual celebrity and someone important, I would like you to give me an explanation on how you got on this ship."

Tanu cackled. "Well, I threatened your guards by saying I would post an article about you hurting an innocent girl if they tried to block me."

* * *

Back in Angora, there was a little bunny going through a vent in one of the rooms, and out of it emerged a lady who could be easily recognized. It was Ms. Teach. Good news was that the security cameras found her sneaking in. They started to beep and Ms. Teach started walking faster. She then transformed into a Ghost of Doom and broke at least a hundred lights. Most people were eating dinner in the cafeteria and did not know what was happening. Ms. Teach slammed open the door to Terry's office room.

Terry did not know what to do so he just told Ms. Teach, "It is time," hoping that would encourage her to surrender. But when she did not respond, he asked, "How did you find us?" shocked that she had tracked them down.

"I have my sources," she scoffed. "Your little students at Angora aren't as loyal as you think."

The giant robot security guard entered the room. Terry hopped onto it, and they broke one of the office room's walls and escaped from Ms. Teach. At this point, a big earthquake and thunderstorm started. But the robot Terry was on grew in size and projected a big shield over all of Angora.

The robot now looked like a dinosaur. It was green, had sharp teeth and a very long tail. The tail was about one hundred times the size of Angora. The dinosaur started shooting lightning at Ms. Teach who had followed Terry outside, but the thunderstorm was getting worse. Magic bombs were dropping from the sky. Terry kept on using the dinosaur's shield to block the bombs but Ms. Teach now had more time to get back into Angora.

Ms. Hopkins, who was inside Angora, suddenly had a feeling that Matthew and the others were in danger. "I better check on the kids in the Rainbow of Glee. The rest of you try to protect Angora," she said as she teleported out.

That was when Matthew awoke with a yelp. He could sense something was wrong and reached out to shake Isabelle and Michael awake.

Suddenly, they heard whispers. "Death is coming. Now. Death... Now...."

Matthew shivered. "We have to go see for ourselves who is

out there. We can't stay under these trees forever."

Michael got up silently and stretched out a hand to Isabelle. The three of them walked along until they were out of the row of trees and in an open area. Right in front of them stood the group J kids (the jokers and bullies).

"Do not worry. The fight will be against more than just the few of us," said a tall boy. Michael squinted his eyes at him. "Alexander," he said loudly. "What are you doing here? How did you find us?"

Alexander snickered. "Don't think getting us expelled got rid of us forever. It is easy to bust people out of jail. Ms. Teach was always good to us so we are following her example. You will die. But you won't be the only ones, ha-ha-ha. Forget 'An-gora'. Soon it will be known as 'Done-gora'."

CHAPTER TEN

THE DESK OF DOOM

As Victoria was digging around in the sand pit, Tom was whining. "This is such a waste of time! My brother is lost, and you are digging holes everywhere."

Victoria snapped her head towards Tom. "I only have to dig a hole in one place because then I can use my detector spell to see if he is underground and see if he is north, south, west, or east."

She dug the rest of the hole faster but felt like she was losing power and energy. Once she put her hand at the bottom of the hole, she yelled the word, "Kjiro!" She heard the trumpeting vibrations with her hand. She stared at Tom. "He is over the ground," she said with some relief. "He isn't buried underneath at least."

She glanced towards her wand. "Oh, no. He is east of us. He is in trouble. Tom, he's stranded in the ocean somewhere."

* * *

As the three kids were staring at the bullies, Matthew saw something unbelievable. A dragon! "You have a dragon?" he asked Alexander, astonished.

Alexander nodded. "He will be part of our fight. Once he wakes up, he will be full of energy - energy to kill you. You see, you might be a Nature Spirit, but the thing is, you can only have untamed animals on your side. And this dragon is tamed and mine!"

Michael stared at Alexander. "You taught the dragon bad things?" he asked but the question was more like a statement. Alexander snickered. "More than just bad things, I taught him how to rule the world. He will listen to none but his master. And once he awakens, what if he doesn't see his master?"

He looked at another male bully. "Tell them what happens. You have felt the pain of it once, Steve."

Steve nodded. "He will kill you. Or at least try to. I barely escaped!" There was a frown curled up on his face and his puffy red cheeks were glowing as he clenched his fists.

Alexander then blew a whistle he took from his pocket. The dragon got up and stared at Matthew. "Kill him!" exclaimed Alexander. Matthew did not know how to protect himself, but he did not want to retreat. The dragon was rainbow colored. In a blur of colors, he charged at Matthew.

Matthew was frozen like a sitting duck, so Michael pushed him out of the way. The dragon grew taller and taller as lava came out of its mouth. Matthew ran up to him. He yelled, "Ravysho!" But for some reason the spell backfired. It came back at Matthew and hit him in the chest. He remembered what Terry had taught him.

"Never use the spell against nature," he recalled him saying. Matthew felt like he was drowning in the deep end of water. He couldn't even open his eyes. He had a shooting pain in his chest and felt a lump of fire growing in his throat. He just...fell. The dragon was standing right over him and nodded his head at Alexander. "I do feel a bit amused on how I trained a dragon to literally talk to me," Alexander told Isabelle and Michael.

Matthew was still in deep shock. As the dragon shot more fire, he felt his heart burning more and more. Matthew couldn't feel his legs to stand up. His body was completely numb.

He didn't have the energy to try any spells. It was no use. "Now, do not worry. I'll be taking the final hit," said Alexander pointing his wand at Matthew's body. "You do not understand any secrets, but your life will be a victory for Group J. We will rise from the ashes."

Michael tried to run to Alexander, but another bully named Taj started sprinting towards him. Michael put his hands up as a sign he had given up. He got chained and handcuffed.

Isabelle was looking at one of the bullies and quietly whispered, "Pretend you are fighting with me." They battled each other, but were mostly pretending to throw punches, though of course Matthew and Michael did not know this. Suddenly, Matthew used all of his energy to open his eyes slightly.

Alexander grinned and Matthew saw his yellow teeth. Michael saw him pull out a golden necklace from his dragon and whispered the words, "Jagam." The necklace turned into something bigger. It became a desk. Alexander tapped the desk gently and opened a drawer and pulled out a piece of paper. It had a code written on it. This was when he looked at Michael and told Taj, "Turn him around." Taj kicked him, and a bit of blood trickled out of a cut in

Michael's back.

Alexander quickly entered the code into a screen resting on the desk. A drawer popped open and out of it came a wand. He looked at the wand. "I can easily do it now, but I need to know the *exact* new location of Angora. Before, I chose the best time to get arrested because I had enough secrets to pass on, and the blackout had almost arrived. This wand as you can see, if you have your eyes open, is a diamond wand with crystals at the top. So, prepare to be hit by the Wand of Secron. You may have avoided the hit on the battlefield but now you will pay." He fixed his eyes on Matthew's face and yelled, "Astro."

The spell hit Matthew in the tummy. His eyes burned and Michael gasped as he saw Matthew's eyes turn red. Matthew could see a picture of Mr. Fire falling in a pit. He tried focusing his mind on finding the strength to escape, but each time it got worse. He now saw his dad falling from the sky.

"You could have saved him if you had given up and not tried to fight me," said a raspy voice. Then he saw Tyron drowning in an ocean. "You could have saved him too," the voice taunted him.

Matthew was so angry with himself for not being strong enough to do anything. Alexander looked at him and snarled, "You might think you are helping the world, but you are just losing more people one by one. Say goodbye to your life." He pointed the Wand of Secron at him again. Matthew could not budge even a bit. "You are weak, Matthew," he chuckled and raised his arm.

Matthew stopped thinking of the past and the future, and just focused on the present. He got up inch by inch, using every bit of energy he could find.

Alexander was watching. "You are wasting so much effort. But I am tired of people saving you just when I have you in my claws. I must destroy you once and for all. Agman!" The spell came speeding toward Matthew who dropped down at the last second. It hit right behind him.

Now in an even angrier tone Alexander yelped, "Agman." This time the spell was certain to hit Matthew and he did not have time to get up. He did the one thing he could. He had only a couple of seconds to react, so he reached into his pocket and held up an object with a flashing red light. It was the Scuba Cube, which deflected the spell. It heated up and he quickly threw it on the ground. Matthew winced looking at his burning fingers but was happy that he was not dead. As Alexander examined the Scuba Cube, Matthew had ten seconds to get up.

"What is this object? How was it able to stop magic?" Alexander stared at Matthew and said, "I have just one word for you. Death!"

Matthew stared back at him, confident now. "Yeah, but wasn't that what you were trying to do for the past, I don't know, ten minutes? Trying to bring about my death?"

* * *

Terry was still fighting Ms. Teach. Several crocodiles came out of her wand. "Ha! The advantages of being a Nature Spirit," she said.

The crocodiles were running around, and all the students

started going crazy.

"Ms. Teach, give up. The only reason you have any strength now is because you have Hornet on your side." It was one of the first times Terry had said that name out loud.

Ms. Teach seemed more angry than surprised. "I've earned what I have. It just so happens that Hornet trusts me and that gives me more confidence. I am evil on my own and I want to be evil. It is my destiny to be evil."

Terry had started writing a message on a post-it note, and once he finished, the note walked straight to Ms. Ivan. "We are going to a new location," she whispered to one child. "Tell everyone else and close the door. Ms. Teach cannot know."

The crocodiles were climbing up Terry's machine. They destroyed the glass window, but Terry simply said, "Morfia," and they were blasted out.

Ms. Ivan had the instructions in her hand so when all the children were gathered together, they started to seal any entrances into Angora. But the plan was not so simple. Some crocodiles were managing to get into the school.

* * *

Tanu flounced onto the red velvet chair and exclaimed, "I really feel the warmth of this seat."

Goliath stared at her. "I said I do not like you and I have a glue gun pointed at you."

Tanu seemed unfazed. "So? You are just risking your own skin. Jack, tell us about your company."

Jack was startled by Tanu's request, but he decided to open up. "Goliath, I would feel a lot more comfortable if you put down that thing. Okay, so my company was first owned by my father. It was called Build High. But once he died it was passed on to me. And I will drill Antarctica to build lots of factories, just as he wished."

Tanu followed up eagerly. "Right, now I need more details that nobody knows yet. I want to include something spicy for the story I am writing about your drilling and factories."

Jack shook his head. "I have secrets that are not to be revealed. Now is not the time for a story."

Goliath was getting restless and spoke up. "And I have secrets to tell you as well. Be thankful that I am telling you this before Alissa does, because her husband is alive and has powers."

Tanu raised her eyebrows with interest. "Powers. Now, do you have any proof of this?"

"The proof is me standing here," responded Goliath. "I was running away from Hornet and his goons – he had mind-controlled the entire police at that point - and I fell off a cliff. The next thing I know, I'm here in Antarctica. I need to get back home and find my son."

Jack raised his hand. "She is telling the truth. I always had a suspicion that Alissa knew more about my brother-in-law Hornet than she was letting on."

Tanu nodded thoughtfully. "So, should these secrets be private? Doesn't the world deserve to know that Hornet has powers?"

Goliath released a long breath. "Well, I think we need to be careful. Hornet is evil and we don't know what he's going after. The more information we can gather first, the better."

Tanu tapped her pen on her book and said, "I understand. But I must tell you that as a journalist, at some point I will be obliged to share these secrets with the world." She paused. "Okay, this is enough information for one day. I am going to explore a bit and then rest." With that, she got up and walked away confidently without looking back.

* * *

Tom started speaking to the ocean. "You are kind. Release my brother," he whispered, but a giant wave emerged and missed Victoria and Tom by only a few yards.

Victoria whipped her head around and glared at Tom. "We cannot get it to listen to us like that. We need an actual plan." She got up and looked at the sea.

"We can't change the past like this. It will affect all timelines in the future. Time traveling is super dangerous. We have to take this seriously. We cannot get caught by anything, especially the lobster crabs on the east side. Those are forbidden. Really! They made such a big impact on history, and it will change if we are caught there. In fact, I hope your brother is safely at sea on the east side." She started walking quickly. "We need a way to transport through the ocean! Any ideas?"

Tom thought for a few seconds, then spoke up. "A surfboard! We can make one!"

Victoria brought out her wand and gave it a little spin. A surfboard appeared. "When you are in the past, the best thing to do is to teleport objects from the future, like this surfboard."

Tom was impressed. He gave a sigh of relief. "Okay great, but I'm not sure I know how to surf."

Victoria was already prepared to show him. "Do not worry. All set," she said as she threw the board into the ocean and jumped on.

* * *

Mrs. Daniel frantically looked for the store Brown had told her about. She had to find someone named Stein who could help track down her husband. As she walked into the store, she saw a sign that said "AMC." "Amazing Machine Crazy. That must be what it stands for," she thought with confidence, and she walked in and saw a small timid man.

"Hello, welcome to our store. Can I help you find a favorite movie classic?"

Mrs. Daniel started to stiffen up. "I need a tracker," she squeaked, unsure of what to say. The man looked at her as though she was crazy.

"I am Stein. I'm sorry but I do not know what you mean. How about you watch the *Three Little Hogs* (remix of three little pigs), it will be fun," exclaimed Stein, and smiled right after. It was obvious that Stein was desperate to have someone buy the movies in his store.

Mrs. Daniel stared at him. She had completely forgotten the

reason why she had come here in the first place. "No way! The book *Three Little Hogs* is way better than the movie, I am not watching it," grunted Mrs. Daniel.

Stein too started to babble. "No! You know the movie has a 100% rating on Rotten Tomatoes, right?" he asked. Mrs. Daniel rolled her eyes.

"Actually, I'm here to see you," she said, suddenly serious. "I need your help desperately. My house is destroyed, and I don't have anybody I can trust. I know you were good friends with Jordan. Can I please request your help finding him and also moving to another house?"

Before Stein could react, someone walked into the store. It was Hornet. "Hello. I have been waiting to see you, Mrs. Daniel. I heard about the baby. Congrats."

Mrs. Daniel looked at him confused. "Who are you? How do you know about my baby? Wait, are you Melissa's father? She looks like you. I heard you were back. Everyone thought you were dead."

Hornet walked right up to her and looked her in the eyes. "Just call me if you need anything, because I am here to help."

* * *

Alexander started to pounce on Matthew. "You might have the power to annoy me, but the thing is I do not fear little kids."

Matthew was about to deflect his attack when another bully also punched him from behind. This bully pointed his wand at Matthew. Then a third bully came from above. And they both seemed to have some muscle.

Alexander laughed. "A three-sided attack. You won't stand a chance. Isabelle is fighting, Michael is chained, and three bullies are after you!" They all angled their wands at Matthew. But Matthew did not move or say a word. He dropped his wand.

"Strength is not the power you possess but the power you find in yourself." Matthew picked up his wand and threw it to Alexander. "You can kill me if that is your heart's desire." Matthew even took off his shoes and socks. "I do not need objects to fend for me. I need just myself!" he yelled.

Alexander chuckled. "Really? You think I will not hurt you just because you're acting naive and brave? Ha!" He lifted his wand. "You are not as wise as the Principal."

"I don't have to be," replied Matthew. "Sometimes even Terry makes mistakes."

"Your words mean nothing," screamed the bully attacking from behind.

Michael's eyes were drooping, and his mouth was closed. "There are amazing things in places you won't expect. Like right in front of you." Matthew put out his hand and yelled the words, "GO!!!" The golden trees swooshed their way into the big cave. Light started to shine as though there was a block of sun lighting up in the darkest place, like a ray of hope.

"Oh no! Run!" shouted a bully. Then, Alexander saw he had two wands, one of which was Matthew's. "No, we're going to destroy each tree piece by piece," he growled. But the second he said that he bumped into Ms. Hopkins.

"Yeah, but first let me take you down piece by piece," said Ms. Hopkins.

Matthew felt a jolt of joy in his body that he had not felt for a long time.

Ms. Hopkins pointed her wand at the bullies. "Escavor," she snarled in a quiet tone. When the bullies jumped out of the way, they started to laugh.

"I heard that was the same spell that killed your mother," said Alexander with an evil grin. "And your necklace that you find so soothing...We are one step ahead of you. Under Ms. Teach's orders we've put a second spell on that necklace."

Suddenly, Isabelle ran to Ms. Hopkins. She did not attack though. The bullies were confused as Isabelle stood protecting her.

"LEAVE HER ALONE!" Even Alexander was scared by her yell. Quietly she added, "Ms. Hopkins. I can undo the curse on your necklace. I know the spell."

Matthew took the opportunity to run towards the bullies. "What are you doing? You are still outnumbered!" yelled one of them.

That was when the tree released one of its branches and picked Alexander up. It threw him against the cave wall. The tree seemed to nod at Matthew and start throwing the other bullies around too.

While the bullies were being dealt with, Isabelle cracked her knuckles. "You just need to trust me. Do not be stiff. Relax..."

Ms. Hopkins could not do this. "I cannot relax! Panic, panic,

panic, panic," she started to mutter.

"No!" shouted Isabelle holding her hands. "I know how you feel. But think about something that makes you happy. Like the first time you stepped into Angora. Relax."

Ms. Hopkins closed her eyes and her tight neck and shoulders started to loosen. "I am ready," she finally decided.

Isabelle nodded. "Hertennbal."

The necklace was peeling off. Ms. Hopkins did not feel the heaviness on her chest anymore. She really felt free and smiled at Isabelle with admiration. "I cannot thank you enough. I will figure out a way to repay you for your kindness."

* * *

Jack was sitting in his drill rig, next to his assistant, Leroy. He was typing on his computer, and there was a wire connected to his Scuba Cube. Jack frowned. "Heard the news that Jordan escaped "prison"?" he asked, referring to his home as the prison.

Leroy nodded. "Yes, I also heard that Melissa freed him," he said. Jack grunted with frustration.

"What are you doing?" asked Leroy. Jack kept on typing letters and numbers into the computer. "I am trying to see Matthew and Mr. Daniel's passports, birth certificates, etc."

After a minute of waiting patiently, Jack finally got all the information he was looking for. Leroy clapped his hands, impressed. "How did you get all that so quickly?" he asked. Jack chuckled.

"I did nothing, Jordan played into the trap. When he was testing the Scuba Cube, I got copies of his retinal scan and fingerprints. He forgot to delete it from the Scuba Cube, and I've held on to it," Jack explained. "And I see something that might not seem important but probably is. Matthew is going to have a little brother."

Leroy's eyebrows started to twitch. "Really?" he asked.

Jack nodded. "In the future, knowing this may come in handy. As of now, you are going to find Melissa and Jordan Daniel, and take care of them!" he bellowed.

Leroy jumped back. "You mean...?"

"She betrayed me. Scare her and shake her up but leave her unharmed. As for Jordan, capture him, but if he resists, then you know what to do." Leroy nodded, signaling that he understood.

* * *

As Tom and Victoria stood on their surfboards, they felt light on their feet. Victoria saw a small island. "We'll get off there and search for Tyron," she said as she looked behind them. "Good. Nothing of concern is behind us. But, uh oh.... The lobster crabs. Quiet," she whispered. The crab was getting closer and closer to them. "Quick, we have to swim to that island," she said looking at it. "We're attracting too much attention on these surfboards."

Then she gasped. "No! The lobster crabs aren't heading towards us. They're heading to the island. It's their territorial base!" But it was too late to turn back. They jumped off their surfboards and started to swim. Once they got to the island, they looked around and were relieved not to see any lobster crabs on the beach.

"Good. Looks like the lobster crabs are not home yet." But she spoke too soon. At least 100 lobster crabs started marching along the sand. "Oh no! They are going to follow us," Victoria said, panicked.

But Tom was just smiling happily. He squinted towards the sunlight and saw that the lobster crabs were carrying Tyron. "Tyron, my brother is alive," said Tom in amazement as he ran with his arms outstretched. Tyron had also noticed Tom, so he jumped off the crabs and started running towards him. But neither of them stopped running and they bumped into each other. They fell down laughing.

"I missed you. The lobster crabs were nice but not as nice as you," Tyron said sweetly. Tom smiled and gave his brother one more hug. Tyron addressed Victoria. "Thank you, too. I would have never been saved if it weren't for you." He hugged her.

"It is still not over," said Victoria. "We have to flash forward to the present day." Tyron looked at them. "I cannot believe I am suggesting this, but I think we should bring several of the lobster crabs with us too. We do not know what we are up against in Angora, and we can use all the help we can get."

Victoria raised her eyebrows, surprised at this suggestion. "That might disrupt events in the timeline. And they are not good fighters. The three of us traveling to the past is bad enough, but bringing them back to our home in the future? I do not think so."

Tyron sighed, trying to find the right words. "I do not think this will change the course of history. The crabs did not do much besides become extinct at some point. But they have the potential to help us."

Victoria took a deep breath in and shook her head. "It is the craziest idea I've ever heard. You just cannot flash anything forward from the past."

Then Tom saw something. Like a sail in the water that was moving. "Um...Were there sailboats in the year 10,000?" he asked, seeing the blue colored sail.

Victoria looked closely to where Tom was pointing and almost fainted. "Ok! This is the end of our lives. As well as those of the lobster crabs. We're looking at the reason they became extinct.

It's the magic Megalodon."

They watched, frozen in place, as the blue sail Tom had spotted started getting bigger and bigger as it came close to shore. It was a giant prehistoric shark that started charging at them.

"We are leaving this area now," said Tom. He started taking giant steps backwards. The big blue creature was coming closer as he was blending in with the blue sea and it was difficult to spot him.

"No, Tom. You cannot escape or defeat it. I mean you could, but that would require a whole different level of power. This Megalodon is a key part of history," Victoria said tearing up. "We won't survive this."

Tyron then shared an idea. "Go! Run up the rocks to the highest point on the island. I'll get the lobster crabs to safety and distract the Megalodon."

Tom shook his head. "If we are doing something, let's do it together. I'm not letting you out of my sight."

"Okay, let's go," replied Tyron. "These crabs can feel the Megalodon's vibrations and are starting to run up the beach. Round them up."

Tom and Victoria nodded as they started gathering the crabs in one area. But the Megalodon spotted them and started to come closer. They got a full view of its razor-sharp teeth, dark black eyes, and blue body. It leapt into the air and seemed to be diving straight at them.

"Oh no," thought Tom. "This is it. We're going to die." Victoria brought out her wand. "We have to try something. Flamero!"

she shouted and got fire into the Megalodon's mouth. "The simplest spells can often be the most effective," she observed as she ran up a hill towards Tom and Tyron.

"We have to win this battle," she yelled. The Megalodon dipped into the water to put out the fire and the force shook the island.

"Oh no," exclaimed Tyron . He saw one lobster crab slip into the water. He was going to save it when Tom stopped him. "It is the circle of life," he said. Tyron looked at the hopeless crab and a tear fell from his eye. The Megalodon was now going for Victoria, and she didn't see any choice but to jump into the water.

Tom was shaking but felt he had to do something. Victoria was sinking into the water and the Megalodon was thrashing around, trying to find her. Tom could not even see its sail as it moved deep underwater. He glanced one more at the lobster crabs that were steadily moving up the hill and ran into the water.

He yelled the words, "Jas," and suddenly he was as fast as a sailfish, and he dove in. Building up momentum, he grabbed the sail of the Megalodon. He held on to it with one hand and with the other he pinched the tip really hard. The Megalodon started straining to go deeper and Victoria still hadn't emerged back up. It was now hard for the Megalodon to change directions since its sail worked to help with steering. Finally, the Megalodon flung Tom off with its tail. And yes, it had a tail as well. It was completely green with big lumpy scales like that of a dragon. Then the craziest thing happened. Without wings, the Megalodon lifted off the water and started to fly.

At the same time, Victoria torpedoed out of the water, coughing but okay. "This complicates things," she said when she caught her breath. She stared at its tail and noticed that the Megalodon's power seemed to be emerging from there. So, she angled her wand towards the tail, but the Megalodon was flying in circles without staying still.

Tyron had moved up the island at this point, leading all the lobster crabs towards the rocks at the top. Tom wished he could be with his brother, but he couldn't leave. "I have to help Victoria," he thought to himself. "I can't leave her here to die."

* * *

Meanwhile, Terry received a message on a magic post-it note: Coordinates A.3958329JGKLS. The Principal pressed the white button on the robot. "Enter Coordinates" showed up on the machine. The Principal looked down at his post-it note and typed it in. Soon the ground started to shake tremendously, teleporting him and Angora away to a new destination.

* * *

Mr. Fire and Jason were walking in the forest. "Why aren't we seeing Angora?" asked Jason.

Mr. Fire signaled for him to stand still and pointed to an area in the distance where there was dust and a rumbling sound. "That is why," he said. "There is something going on in Angora right now so it's safest we observe it from here."

Once the earthquake stopped, Mr. Fire and Jason spotted the cheetahs. "The monster that was by the Haspura rock does not seem too angry now," said Jason smiling. Unfortunately, they were stuck in enemy territory.

In Angora's new location, Ms. Ivan went up to Terry looking terrified. "Mr. Fire is still missing along with a number of our students. Ms. Hopkins is missing as well."

Terry gulped. "Where are they?! The students promised me they would be back soon. How could this happen?"

Ms. Ivan turned as white as ghost as she saw Terry's expression. "I have no idea..."she said.

* * *

Isabelle snuck out of the cave as the others were resting and saw a little pond of water. She stared into it and saw a reflection of Ms. Teach, Hornet, and the bullies.

"Sorry I could not kill him, father," said Isabelle.

Hornet looked at her proudly. "You did perfectly fine. In fact, better than fine. Ms. Teach, you too. Alexander could have done better though. Isabelle, you earned Ms. Hopkins' trust. Angora will soon be within reach. Ms. Teach, you made them shift their Angora location twice. This is good...They are vulnerable every time they move to a new location. I do not only want to conquer Angora, but I also want to conquer the entire Magic World. I think we need to meet in person to plan things out. Isabelle, I will meet you in Ecuador. Await my instructions. Bullies, you did not kill Matthew like I asked. I have to say you did a very poor job. But I have another plan in place. I have captured Adam, Matthew's best friend. I have threatened him already. If he doesn't cooperate, I will capture Adam's mom. And I will have the power to control her mind."

* * *

Again, Tom tried to jump onto the flying shark's back. The shark was starting to spray water from its mouth and Victoria pointed her wand at it. "Arisol!" she yelled.

Tom started to go faster once more so he could reach the height of the flying Megalodon, but he saw something in his way. "Um... Victoria this might hurt but I'll have to bump into you!"

Victoria started to laugh thinking Tom was joking but he was telling the truth. He tried to slow down but he hit Victoria and started to fly up in the sky. He luckily landed on the giant Megalodon's head. He felt the sun burning against his cheeks.

"Eeeeek!" the Megalodon screeched. He wobbled his head in an attempt to eat Tom, or at least knock him off his head.

Tom looked into the Megalodon's mouth and all he could see was teeth. He pointed his wand there. The shark was about to chomp down on the wand, but Tom threw it into his mouth.

The Megalodon froze and was as still as a sloth as Victoria yelled, "Flamero!" The spell hit his tail. The shark was in shock, as he glared at Tom and Victoria, and then closed his eyes as though ready for a nap.

They stared at each other. "Wow!" Tom chuckled, "It looks like you got him to relax. By the way, I was expecting the shark to be way smaller than it actually is."

Victoria nodded. "I know what you mean. Listen, this may sound crazy, but I know exactly how to get back to present day. Tell

Tyron that we are jumping into the Megalodon's mouth! It's a portal...If we miss this chance who knows when we'll next be able to get out of here."

Tom's mouth flew open, but he saw her serious expression and swallowed hard. "Wow...I'm not even going to ask how you know this stuff. Okay, I'll signal to Tyron to come down from the hill." The Megalodon in the meantime continued to be calm, like he had been tamed by the spell. When Tyron came with the lobster crab army, they hopped into the shark's mouth hoping Victoria was right. Within a second, they were blasted into the present, right next to Matthew.

"Matthew!" gasped Tyron as they appeared. Matthew was sitting outside the cave. "Hi guys! How did you escape?" asked Matthew excitedly. Tom explained the whole situation then asked, "Have you found your dad?"

Matthew shook his head. "We had to battle the bullies. It looked like they were expecting us to come here. I'm just glad Tyron was located."

Matthew was staring into the river when he said, "I can't even communicate with my mom to see how she's doing. I don't have a Scuba Cube anymore." A single teardrop fell into the river. "The bullies were there. Isabelle saved Ms. Hopkins. Nothing makes sense." He took a coin from his pocket and threw it into the river and Tom wondered if he was making a wish. The sun was shining brightly.

He sighed and continued speaking "I don't know what I'm doing. I've failed on this mission. I can't find my dad and I'm putting everyone around me in danger. What do I do next?"

Ms. Hopkins and Michael approached them. She had seen him throw the coin into the water "This is the river of hatred. Never give it your respect or it will bite back at you," Ms. Hopkins said.

"What does it matter at this point...I've given up trying," said Matthew sadly.

Ms. Hopkins pulled Matthew away from the water. "You have to be strong. Don't believe what you saw and heard when you were with Alexander. I know he got into your head. You may have seen your father falling from the sky, but he is not dead. But you can't stay here. This river will poison you, especially if you have the curse of Karkatu."

Matthew had a glum expression. "What is the curse?"

Ms. Hopkins looked down at her shoes, trying to find the best way to explain what these words meant.

"It is generally forbidden to talk about the curse, because of how Karkatu betrayed my mother. This river was made for communication with others, but it is dangerous because of what it can make you feel and think. Like the way Alexander made you imagine your father falling. It also gives out fake prophecies which trick our mind into thinking they are real. Ms. Teach received a fake prophecy and was tricked by Karkatu. This is why she is so angry all the time. Karkatu is responsible for killing my mother. Ms. Teach - my own sister - now hates him. But she didn't listen to my warnings. Ms. Teach now wants to wage the first war of Karkatu, for revenge. She even came up with a fake name to disguise herself at Angora so no one would know who she really is. It all came to my head the second the blackout hit. This is when I saw Ms. Teach with my necklace. I realized she had joined Hornet because he is so powerful, and he has the ability to outsmart me. Or at least he thinks he does. But she does not know that the decision is going to destroy her. She's my sister and I want to help her, but I don't know if I can. I wonder what my mom would do if she was alive. Matthew, please do not look in that river and do not think of Hornet or Alexander's special wand which has power over you. Let it go."

* * *

Isabelle was sitting down with the special wand and thought about everything that her father Hornet had said.

"I'll make sure to give this wand to my father. And I have to go to Ecuador in the Non-Magical World. How genius of him, but why has he asked me to go tomorrow? I guess he doesn't want to waste any time," she thought and got up when she saw Ms. Hopkins in front of her.

"Thank you for all your help. Now let's go back to Angora. Although we haven't found Matthew's father, this trip was not a waste as it has given me a lot to think about. Let me follow your way out of this portal," Ms. Hopkins stated.

Isabelle nodded, pleased that Ms. Hopkins trusted her. They followed their footprints back to the portal, saying goodbye to each golden tree, although Matthew could not see the one that had saved him.

As he was walking away, he heard a whisper. One of the small golden trees raised its branch. "Don't lose hope, Matthew. Your dad is alive in Non-Magic World. I see him outside a mansion with a group of youngsters around your age. He doesn't look happy. He's been through a lot but he's hopeful to be reunited with you and your mom soon."

Matthew had tears in his eyes. "Thank you, my friend," he said to the golden tree. "Be well." Once they got themselves out of the Rainbow of Glee they were on a big rock.

Ms. Hopkins gathered everyone around her. "Okay, now I am going to teleport each of you back to Angora. I'll have to take you one at a time and will teleport back here to take the next student."

Matthew went first because he was the only one that had been teleported by Ms. Hopkins before (when he first came from Non-Magic to Magic World). Then, everyone else was teleported. Once they were on the grass, they felt good but also shaken up. They had made it, yet they felt as though they had broken a few bones along the way.

"Why aren't we in Angora?" asked Ms. Hopkins, puzzled. Right next to her was Mr. Fire and Jason. Everyone looked happy to see each other and Mr. Fire filled them in on the earthquake they had seen earlier right where Angora used to stand. As the group discussed ideas to locate Angora, the giant rocks lying ahead of them started to shift.

Victoria immediately pulled out her wand and pointed it at the rocks, worried about what was going to happen next. As they watched, the demon emerged from the rocks. She started to laugh. "It's a pity there is so much destruction in one place. First the earthquake and now me. I, the Weather Lord's assistant, am here to fight you. All trees must be destroyed, so the Nature Lord Karkatu will never return. Join me and your sister and forget about Angora." More lightning struck.

"How can she control nature if she is not the Nature Lord? What is going on?!" asked Jason looking terrified.

The green monster heard him and laughed. "I have your friend Matthew to thank for that. When I'm near a Nature Spirit, I can channel his or her powers and control nature as well. Now answer me, Ms. Hopkins. Are we going to destroy Karkatu together?"

Ms. Hopkins shook her head.

"Then I'll be forced to kill you," responded the demon. She shot green vines from her palms, but Matthew jumped in front of Ms. Hopkins. The vines stopped when they were a few inches away from him.

"What?" she screeched. "Impossible."

"Not really," said Ms. Hopkins. "You forgot one key detail. You and my sister think alike. She is willing to share her powers with you. But Matthew is pure and honest. These traits make him very different from you and block your ability to channel his powers."

The demon looked defeated. She vanished without another word.

* * *

Right at that moment, Adam was sitting with the stone in his hand, trying to figure out a way to keep it away from Hornet. Hornet was on the other side of the room. "We will take a yacht to Ecuador. We

217

need to get there in a day."

Adam shook his head. "I am not going. Why would I go? You've captured me, controlled the police and you expect me to follow."

Hornet looked at him and hiccupped nervously. "I need you because of your so-called friend. And although you are Non-Magical, I know your mother. If you want to keep her safe, I suggest you cooperate without a fuss." Adam stayed silent and Hornet continued.

"I have one kid stranded in Magic World and one in Non–Magic world. When I left my wife Alissa all those years ago, she didn't even know that I had left for good until a day or two later. Now that I'm back I need to get them on my side before they realize my scheme against Angora. It was my plan to lure Alissa and Melissa to Helen's house and talk to them together there."

* * *

Ms. Hopkins clapped her hands. "Now that we got rid of the demon, let's focus on finding Angora."

Jason was confused but let go of his confusion because he did not want Ms. Hopkins to panic even more. Then they saw Tyron staring at something on the ground. It was a magic post-it note that said, **Coordinates A.3958329JGKLS.**

"What is this?" asked Tyron.

Ms. Hopkins looked at what Tyron was pointing to and smiled, and in the next few minutes the entire group was flying towards their destination, with the same queasy feeling as before. They landed in the new location of Angora right outside Terry's office.

Terry ran outside to greet them. "Hello, welcome back! I'm glad you're all okay. We left the magic post-it note near our old location and programmed it with your descriptions so it would find you." He listened patiently as they filled him in on their adventures. Matthew apologized for the way they left Angora and sadly reported that they failed to find his father.

Terry put his hand on Matthew's shoulder to console him. "I am happy to see you, just not happy to hear the news you have reported. But I will continue to ask my friends in security to let me know if they hear anything about your father."

Ms. Hopkins looked at the Principal. "Also, I wanted to tell you something about Isabelle. She was a courageous and wise leader on our trip and should be recognized for saving the day. If it weren't for her, we would all be dead meat."

Terry nodded kindly at Isabelle. "You know, you remind me of a friend of mine, Isabelle. Leading your friends to safety, you look like someone I knew a long time ago - Hornet - but your heart is pure unlike him. I trust you, Isabelle. Now go on and get some fresh air," he concluded as he stood up and left the office.

Isabelle cheeks turned red with all the compliments. "Ms. Hopkins, I am so tired. Can I just sit here for a few minutes before I move again?"

Ms. Hopkins looked closely at her. "You do seem tired. Rest up and call me if you need anything. I'm heading back to my room."

Isabelle quickly opened several drawers in Terry's desk and

pulled out some papers. She made copies in the photocopy machine, using a spell to speed up the process. Isabelle quickly put the original papers back. "Secrets dad would love to know...,"she whispered, and she quickly walked out of the office. "The war has just started."

* * *

Despite Jack's request not to share any information about his work, Tanu hosted a virtual meeting for journalists. Jack was so angry, but he couldn't show it in front of everyone. He knew he would lose popularity if he refused to talk. "There is a Magical World," he told himself. "And I need to become famous in both Magic and Non-Magical Worlds." So, he joined the meeting with a smile on his face. Goliath was also invited and was sitting down with a polite expression. Jack could tell that people on the screen were whispering about him. He cleared his throat. "Thank you everyone for joining this meeting. I wanted to explain a few things to all of you. You may think I am a fool, but my goal is to destroy nature and make money from Magic World. And then destroy it. I see Magic World as a threat to us, just as I see nature as a threat. Once there is no nature and only money for everyone to share, there will be peace."

Tanu glanced at everyone in the meeting who were still glaring at Jack. "Jack, everybody here thinks nature will have to survive because there is a purpose to it."

Jack stared hard at the screen with a determined look in his eye. "What is more fun, watering your plants or burning fossil fuels?"

Suddenly everyone started chanting, "Burning fossil fuels! Burning fossil fuels!" Jack turned to Tanu with a smile on his face.

"She does not want us to have fun doing it. She wants me to lose my purpose so that all of us can see nature tear down our world. The fires, the floods, and the diseases we have because of nature. But if we destroy it, none of this will happen. Now I'll let my smartest scientist explain things in more detail to you."

The scientist with the T-shirt that said **J is for Jack** stepped in front of the screen. He was the one that had made the second sun prediction. "I have invented a machine that will become our ultimate weapon. Based on my observations of the Lava Monsters, I have created a new type of robot that brings together their power and is completely under the control of the Jack Company. It is not ready yet though and is currently a simple robot. Over time I will make it bigger. The robot's heat generates a huge amount of energy. My next step is to test an elephant sized robot filled with lava that can enter a forest and destroy it in a day. All trees will be burnt down. Who cares if there is no clean air? We can still have oxygen tanks so we breathe in pure air and can build more houses and cars and factories with the new space and energy we will have. With these Lava Monsters we will have infinite sources of energy for the robots. All our problems on Earth will be solved. Who is in?"

Tanu shook her head. "No! What you're saying doesn't make sense. Don't—" But she stopped talking when she noticed everyone on screen, and Goliath too, had raised their hands.

Now Jack said a few parting words to the meeting attendees and ended the call. He turned to Tanu. "Tanu, this is the power of a real leader. Your voice is not going to make a difference. I suggest you pack your bags and leave before I'm forced to kick you out."

For once, Tanu didn't have any words. She got up quietly and left.

Now Jack turned to Goliath. "Check on your son Adam. He is headed to Ecuador with Hornet. I see everything, remember that."

CHAPTER ELEVEN

THE HOUSE OF FLOODS

Melissa was planning to sleep over at her grandmother Helen's house. She was going to arrive in an hour, with her friends and Mr. Daniel. The plan was to persuade her grandmother to allow them to use her yacht to meet her father Hornet. Melissa was not aware that her mother Alissa was at Helen's house as well.

As they stood at the front door about to ring the bell, a guard who had been following them from Jack's house saw Mr. Daniel and started to blow his whistle. He had a t-shirt that said **J is for Jack**. "That's the criminal! Mr. Daniel!" he screamed. The guards next to him emerged and started chasing after Mr. Daniel.

"Uh oh!!" Mr. Daniel cried under his breath. He sprinted as fast as he could as Jack's crew got out their guns and started to fire at him. Melissa looked like she wanted to say something, but she knew she could get in huge trouble for helping Mr. Daniel escape. Jack bullets, the deadliest kind, rose in the air and flew towards Mr. Daniel, who had to jump high to avoid them. By this time, all the noise had drawn the attention of Helen's staff. One of Helen's butlers opened the door.

"Hello! What is this racket?" he asked.

"Please let me in," begged Mr. Daniel. "I was taken hostage by someone dangerous."

Melissa immediately chimed in. "Please Yates, believe us, we need to get inside right now. I'll explain later."

The butler looked confused but let the group enter. Jack's guards had been hiding in the bushes and slowly emerged.

Someone in Jack's crew screamed, "Just ring the doorbell geniuses."

A few seconds later the doorbell rang again, and the butler opened the door. "Yes, can I help you?"

The guards didn't know what to say exactly. "We need to speak to the man who just came in. His name is Daniel."

The butler stared at the guards. "I'm sorry, I can't help you. They are meeting with the owner of this house, Ms. Helen. And she doesn't appreciate strangers making strange requests." With that, he shut the door.

They grunted and one of the guards took a step back and called Jack. He spoke to him for a couple of minutes and ended with, "Got it. We'll be in and out. And no one will know you have anything to do with this."

He hung up the phone and spoke to the others. "We break in through the windows. No one is to get hurt – Jack's orders. We just grab Mr. Daniel and leave. Everyone, hold up your guns."

Meanwhile, Mr. Daniel sat next to Helen in a cozy little room. It had red velvet couches and a diamond studded table. "Wow, this room alone probably is worth more than my entire house," thought

Mr. Daniel.

Helen responded sternly, "I'm going to talk to Melissa in a few minutes, but first I need to know who you are and why you are with my granddaughter. Answer me immediately before I call the police."

"My name is Jordan Daniel and I work at the Jack Company with your son. I don't know how to tell you this, so I'll just be honest. Your son is worried I will reveal some of his secrets and locked me up in his house. Luckily, Melissa felt sorry for me and needed my help with something, so she let me escape. She's a good kid. I could have run away as soon as I left Jack's house but wanted to do the right thing and keep my word by helping her out. I'm willing to forgive Jack and won't go to the police, but I need you to trust me on this. I'm about to have a baby and need to get back to my wife."

Helen thought for a minute. "I'm a good judge of character and somehow I do trust you. I recognize your name. You are the lead programmer who designed the Scuba Cube, aren't you?" Mr. Daniel nodded.

She sighed. "I've been worried about my son for a while. He is brilliant but lacks judgement. I don't know why he kept you in his house, but I agree it wasn't the right thing to do. What can I do for you now?"

Mr. Daniel sat up straight. "I know this is a strange request, but we need access to one of your yachts. It is a life-or-death situation and I need to travel to Ecuador tomorrow. I'm sorry I can't tell you more, it's top secret. I don't know if you heard, but my son Matthew is in trouble. I need to help him." Mr. Daniel looked miserable and hated lying to Helen, but he didn't know how else to handle the situation. He had promised Melissa he would help get her a yacht for her journey.

Helen looked confused. "I don't understand how my granddaughter is caught up in all of this. But I know she went to school with Matthew and I'm assuming they were friends." She paused. "I will give you a yacht to use along with a crew tomorrow. But after that, I want you to disappear and not get involved with my family anymore. This means you'll have to resign from the Jack Company if you haven't already. Is that clear?"

Mr. Daniel nodded gratefully. "Yes, I understand."

Meanwhile, Alissa was in the dining room with Melissa. "Mom, how are you here?" she asked as she stared at her mother.

"Well, I got a hologram message from grandma asking me to come here, so I did. It sounded important. Who's the man speaking to grandma?" she asked Melissa.

Melissa didn't want to answer the question, so she pretended to be distracted by her friends. "Let me go check... I need to see where my friends are anyway," she said quickly and joined John, Emily, and Joanne.

She peeked into the living room. "Oh good, Mr. Daniel is talking to grandmother now. I hope he manages to convince her to lend us a yacht. I don't want to interrupt them. Let's go up and wait in the guestroom."

Melissa and her friends were lounging in the guestroom when

they heard a loud crack and one of the windows nearby shattered. Some of Jack's guards entered with guns pointed at the four kids.

"What are you doing?" Melissa screamed. "I'm going to call my uncle right now. How dare you break into my grandmother's house this way."

The guard smirked at her. "Go ahead, call him. Who do you think gave us permission to break in? He wants Mr. Daniel back no matter what the consequences. So, I suggest you and your little friends cooperate with us."

* * *

Terry observed Matthew quietly. "I owe you a spell," he said grimly. "This spell is no joke - it is the third and most serious type of spell. Let me tell you the history of the spell, because that is something most kids do not understand. But Matthew, I know you will. You never had the freedom to go out and explore the world until now."

As Matthew listened Terry continued speaking, "It was my father. He was the non-magical one in my family. It happened when my little brother was off to college. My mother was involved in something I did not want to know about. At least that was what my father said. And he was overprotective of me. I lived near a forest, and he hated nature and said that he never wanted me to go exploring. My mom rarely got a break from work. I could never spend time with her as much as I tried. And then one day, I went outside to meet some friends even though my mom was home, and my dad came after me to convince me to come back. When we both got home, we discovered my mom had died. I could tell what he was thinking. If we had been home, we might have been able to prevent whatever had caused her death. I was young and foolish. I ran away before my father noticed.

"I ran to join my brother in college because I had to do something useful to make up for my guilt. The college asked me for money and some signed papers from my father. I did not have any of it. That was when I met Hornet. He was the best friend you could imagine. He helped me get the money, convinced the college to accept me...Everything was great until he revealed his true colors and backstabbed me at the apartment. C o t m. H n. S e f a m a. K e y t. E t y h m. S t g o t w. This is what he said to me on those final days. It's etched in my mind. I am still thinking of what it stands for. In any case, we came up with two spells together. The one I am about to teach you now was mostly Hornet's creation. Only ones with a pure heart can avoid becoming evil when using this spell. You will be the third person to know it."

Matthew held up his hand and stopped Terry for a few seconds. "I just need to digest all this information before we begin. I feel very lucky that you are teaching me these spells. But I can't get past what I heard you say about being Hornet's friend. Are you still in touch with him? He seems like such an evil person. I think he's responsible for everything that's gone wrong in my life right now. I have no idea where my dad is, and I feel helpless. My mom is by herself, about to have a baby, and I don't know if she's safe. Someone destroyed our house. And when I threw the Scuba Cube to save myself, I lost my only communication link to Non-Magic World. So even though I want to learn this new spell, all I can think about is getting back to my family."

Terry looked startled at the interruption. "Okay, slow down...I understand. You need to help your family. You have to believe me when I say I have nothing to do with Hornet. I wish I knew where he was. But for now, let's work on learning that spell."

* * *

Melissa and the others were scared.

The guard who had threatened them laughed really hard. "You expect you can stop me? I'm Leroy, Jack's best guard."

Suddenly they heard a beeping noise and a hologram popped out of the security camera on the wall. The hologram was of a woman with short brown hair, tan skin, and blue eyes like the color of the ocean. "Intruder!" she yelled. "Activating security protocol. Warning Helen."

Leroy looked unsure for a second then shook his head. "You're too slow," he said as he threw a smoke bomb on the ground. He and his guards escaped out of the window they had just smashed. Melissa started coughing and ran to the window for fresh air. She could see more guards surrounding the house.

She covered her nose and mouth with her shirt sleeve and gestured to the others. "Let's get out of here."

Downstairs, Helen was getting off the phone with her assistant to arrange for the yacht to leave the port the following day. "I have one more favor to ask you, Helen," said Mr. Daniel, looking uncomfortable. "In addition to calling my wife, I need to reach my son. The Scuba Cube is my only chance of communication with him, but I no longer have access to any device."

Helen understood his request. "You may borrow the Scuba Cube my son gave me." She walked over to a bookshelf and brought down a Scuba Cube that looked almost brand new. Helen handed it to Mr. Daniel. "Call your family."

Suddenly, they heard a big BOOM. "I do not like the sound of that," said Mr. Daniel. A few seconds later an alarm started to sound, and a hologram appeared in the room. "Helen, move to safety. The house is under attack."

Helen looked panicked. "My daughter Alissa! And where are Melissa and her friends? Mr. Daniel, I need you to help me find them and bring them to safety." Mr. Daniel looked longingly at the front door and wondered if this was his chance to quickly escape. But as he saw Helen's scared expression and thought about Melissa and others needing help, he nodded.

Melissa started to sprint down the stairs. She wanted to get out of the house as quickly as she could and escape. Then, she saw her mother in the kitchen confused and disoriented. "Mom!" Melissa yelled, "We have to get out of here. These guys are claiming to be from Uncle Jack's company. They've surrounded the house and are trying to hurt us."

Alissa gasped and ran after Melissa as they dashed towards the exit. "Where's grandma?" asked Alissa looking around.

"I don't know, her security hologram said it would warn her.

She's not in the living room anymore so I'm hoping she's hiding somewhere safe," commented Melissa.

Jack's guards were stationed outside looking up at the windows. "We need to make this quick," said Joanne. "Hopefully they won't expect us to run out the back door." She opened the door but Melissa pushed her aside so she could be up front. They started tiptoeing out when suddenly a guard saw them. Before he could act, Melissa zapped him with lightning. He fell and his face looked as if he had just fallen into a black hole. They all hid in a bush. Alissa was shocked at the extent of Melissa's power. There was smoke pouring out of the house as more smoke bombs were thrown inside. Bullets were hitting the house as Leroy waited for Jordan to come out.

* * *

Once Isabelle entered Non-Magic World, she found herself in the United States of America. She consulted the instructions Hornet had sent her. "First stop, get some supplies and cash," she said in a low voice. "Then I book myself on the next flight to Ecuador."

* * *

Meanwhile, in Angora, Terry told Matthew, "This spell is performed differently from 'Ravysho.' Instead of saying it loud and proud, this spell must be softer as though you want to hide it from the world. Like this – 'Ululu'." Terry's tone was soft, yet it rolled off his tongue as swift as a butterfly. Then a little squirt of water came out of his wand and hit Matthew.

Matthew pulled up his wand. "Ululu," he chanted softly but firmly. Everything was as still as before. He gasped. "I think your desk moved a few inches."

Terry sighed. "Mastering a spell created by your arch enemy is hard, but do you know what is harder? Overcoming a fear of hurting someone by accident."

Matthew shrugged not sure what to do next.

Terry gave him some good advice. "This spell may have been made by a bad person, but that does not mean it has to be used for bad things. Hornet was once good – I refuse to believe that all our time as good friends was pretend - but he then turned bad. I've never figured out what triggered the change in his personality. Matthew, you won't turn evil by using this spell, so don't fear it. Just remember to never use the spell against a non-magic person or nature."

Matthew nodded at Terry. He changed the subject, "I just hope my dad isn't trying to contact me right now. Principal Terry, you've done so much for me already, but I need to ask. Do you have a Scuba Cube for me to use?"

Terry hesitated for a moment then opened a drawer in his desk. "Thanks to Brown, we ended up ordering several of these," he said holding up a Scuba Cube. "This one is now yours."

Matthew accepted the device gratefully. "Thank you so much. You don't know what this means to me," he said. "Let me see if there have been any important updates since I last used one of these." He saw a flashing light and pressed face 20 on the Scuba Cube.

A video appeared on the Scuba Cube and Matthew saw Jack trying to look stylish in a suit but instead looked like a bullfrog. "Okay everyone, listen up. There is something going on in the universe that is beyond what we can see with our eyes. The sun is changing, and active scientists have been observing things on the sun that we cannot explain. I have shared pictures of the Lava Monsters with all of you already. We think that these Lava Monsters dropped from the sun to a cold climate because there was an unexpected instant change of weather for five minutes. The good news is we have learned how to control these monsters and use their energy for our benefit. This is the strength of the Jack Company. I have the smartest scientists working for me who will be able to keep us safe and make us more powerful.

"But now we have a problem in our own world. One of my top programmers – Jordan Daniel – has caused some issues for my company and has disappeared. His son Matthew has been tracked down to a different world altogether. The Magic World, as it is known, could be a great threat to those of us on Earth. And as my theory predicted, Matthew was teleported to Magic World. This is a new way of traveling between worlds that we are still trying to understand. But my Scuba Cube can help connect us to that world.

"Magic World - once we find it, we will destroy it, but only after we collect all the precious resources they have. And we can then make Magic World into our own little playground. That is why I would like to present to you my almost finished weapon called The Lava Sector. It will take a few more months to test and get it ready, but it can expand in size and grow in power like no machine you have ever seen before. So, if you'd like to take a risk to get rich, come and join me. Follow the Jack Company!"

Matthew looked at Terry as his body was trembling in fear. He took a deep breath, in and out. "I can't believe he mentioned my dad and me to the whole world. People are going to get the wrong idea about us. Okay, I am ready to learn my spell," he said softly.

Terry put his wand on Matthew's. "You still have room for improvement but for now it is pretty good." He pressed down harder with his wand. "It is clear you have not found your Heart of Magic, Matthew. Someday you will know what it is, and your path will become clearer."

"Say the spell." Terry pointed his wand at Matthew. "I am going to do Ravysho at you, defend yourself." Terry yelled the spell and Matthew could hear his tone so loud that everybody in Angora may have been able to hear it.

"Uluru," said Matthew softly and as rain poured down on Terry's spell, the fire stopped.

Terry nodded with approval, and right after that, Matthew heard a small ringing sound on the new Scuba Cube. Brown was calling him. He accepted it and could feel the vibrations of Brown's heavy breathing on the Cube.

"Hello, Matthew! I just hacked into one of Jack's tracking apps. Mr. Daniel is in Helen's house - that's Melissa's grandmother - and Jack's guards are surrounding it," said Brown, "I first tried your Scuba Cube, which didn't work, but this number did. I was hoping you were near Terry."

A frown curled up on Matthew's face, and he shook his head in disbelief. The golden tree had also said that his dad was in a mansion. It must have been Helen's mansion. "Thank you for telling me this," he said gratefully and hung up. Matthew nodded at Terry. "If I tell you where the house is, will you be able to get me there and then bring yourself back to Angora? When I am at Helen's house, I will hopefully be okay. Jack is no competition against magic. I don't want you to be a target in Non-Magic World. Angora needs you."

Terry chuckled, "I like your confidence. Just remember, you cannot hurt anyone non-magical with magic."

After that, Matthew explained to Terry where Helen's house was, and Terry found the coordinates. "I'll get you there," he promised.

He teleported Matthew a few hundred meters away from the house. Matthew looked at it in awe and jumped back seeing the fire. "Good luck." said Terry and teleported away.

The first guard he really noticed was Leroy. The guard taunted, "Come out, Melissa. Prepare to face your doom."

Matthew knew he might be too late to prevent Helen's house from burning to the ground, but he couldn't turn his back on people in danger. He sprinted up to Leroy and kicked him on the back.

"You really think you are stronger than me?" Matthew scoffed. "This is just to give a taste of what I can do." He pointed his wand at a random angle and yelled, "Ravysho!!" A streak of fire shot out and hit a streetlamp.

He was aware that he could not actually use the spell on Leroy, but he wanted him to feel scared. And the plan worked. Leroy looked terrified and took a step back from Matthew. He gestured to the other guards.

"Forget about the others! Help me attack Matthew!" There was a sudden burst of flames just then and Matthew saw a part of Helen's house starting to collapse. He ran into the house and could feel vibrations of the library shattering into a million pieces. He started to cough and could feel the oxygen level getting lower and lower. "Uluru!" said Matthew without thinking. The house became a swimming pool as the explosives died out.

Matthew saw Mr. Daniel in the corner and swam to him. Mr. Daniel smiled seeing his son. "That's my boy!" he said.

They swam together, trying to find Helen next. Matthew spotted her out of the corner of his eye. She was sitting on a table, holding on tight, as it floated towards them. As he swam towards her, a ripple from behind made the table tip over and she fell into the water. Helen stayed calm and started to doggy paddle in the water. Mr. Daniel helped pull her up.

"Because your house is on a private beach, I guess you're not afraid of the water," he said.

"Humph...I don't want water like this in my house!" Helen remarked. "Melissa and Alissa...Are my girls safe?" she asked.

Matthew nodded. "They're outside, just fine."

He noticed the water level rising in the house and figured a side door would be the easier place to exit from. Matthew signaled to them, and they started to swim in the direction he was pointing. He noticed a room with a carousel and saw the ponies starting to break and get washed up in the water.

"I thought I saw a side door this way, but we've been swimming for a few minutes now. How big is your house exactly?" asked Matthew.

Helen bowed as though it was important to acknowledge this as a compliment. "I don't know, are you asking how many floors I have? Bedrooms? Square feet? But if you're wondering about exits, let's take the one at the back of the house. It leads to the beach."

They got to the exit but saw there was too much water to reach the door handle. "Break the right-side wall now and you will get to the beach," said Helen. So, Matthew broke the wall using Ravysho and they just missed the huge waves from hitting them. They ran outside.

The three of them started to run along the water, their feet creating an imprint on the sand that was washed away the next second. Matthew looked back at the water now gushing out of the house and raised his wand. "Ravysho!" he screamed. But the fire got washed out by the intensity of the water, and Matthew had no spells left to try. He shook his head at Helen and his dad.

"If it keeps on going, we're going to drown!" Mr. Daniel screamed since he didn't want his voice to be swallowed up by the waves.

As the water kept rising, Matthew suddenly thought of an idea. He remembered a spell that Ms. Ivan had taught him about picking up sand. He closed his eyes to recall exactly what the spell was and yelled out, "Shogi!"

Much of the sand on the beach started to rise. He pointed the wand at the house and flicked his wrist. There was a huge woosh and after a few seconds, silence. The sand had succeeded in absorbing all the water. The house was in ruins but at least they were safe.

Matthew took a deep breath in and breathed out slowly. He immediately walked over and hugged his dad, the emotions of the last few weeks pouring out.

As they walked along the beach, Mr. Daniel quickly told Matthew everything, including Jack's role in capturing him and how he ended up at Helen's house. Matthew shared his experiences as well, including his search outside Angora to find him.

"Wow," remarked Mr. Daniel. "We've both been through a lot."

Once they got back to the main entrance of the house, Matthew noticed Melissa, her friends and Alissa were still hiding in a bush, unsure if it was safe to come out. Jack's guards were gone, probably flushed out by the water. But Matthew couldn't believe that Melissa was still here. His arch enemy. It seemed like eternity since they had seen each other.

Suddenly, Leroy jumped out of a bush, his gun pointed at Matthew's heart. He was about to shoot when Matthew used the Ravysho spell to melt his gun. Leroy dropped the gun and screamed. "You will pay for this," he said as he ran away. Matthew reached for his dad's hand and held it tightly.

"Let's go," Matthew said, trying to get away from Melissa. Mr. Daniel stood next to Helen, trying to find the right words. "I am so sorry this happened to your house, Helen. But you need to know something. The truth is, it wasn't me who needed the yacht, it was them." He pointed to Melissa and the others. "They have some travels planned," he said as he walked away quickly. Helen tapped her chin, pondering over what she had just heard.

Alissa, and Melissa ran to Helen and hugged her. "Thank goodness we are all safe!" said Alissa.

Helen looked at them with tears in her eyes. "Is Jack responsible for all of this? What has come over him? All this because of Mr. Daniel?"

Melissa opened her mouth to say something about Mr. Daniel but realized it would only get her in trouble for bringing him here. She stayed silent and Alissa shrugged her shoulders. "I don't know what he's up to," she said quietly.

"And what do you need a yacht for, Melissa?!" questioned Helen, now more angry than anything. Just then Melissa's friends ran up to her and Helen decided to bring this up later. She turned to talk to her security team.

"Maybe I can answer that," said a strange voice that Alissa vaguely recognized.

She turned around and saw her husband Hornet. Alissa gasped.

* * *

Mrs. Daniel was waiting at their house and came rushing out when Matthew and Mr. Daniel arrived.

"I can't believe it! You're both safe and standing here. I'm so happy!" she cried.

Matthew had a huge grin on his face as he hugged his mom tightly. "Let's go inside and talk," he said and started to walk into the house.

There was a giant hole in the living room wall and signs of destruction everywhere. Mrs. Daniel gulped. "Sorry you have to see your home in this state, Matthew."

"I can't believe this," he said. "I knew it was bad. Did they ever figure out who did this?" he asked.

Mr. Daniel looked like he was about to say something, but he stopped. Mrs. Daniel shook her head. "No. But there's more. The insurance company came by, and they will help us relocate to another house. We have three months to pack up and move out of there."

Mr. Daniel shook his head in disbelief. "You're giving up our house without consulting us?"

"You weren't here, Jordan! I had to deal with this by myself!" yelled Mrs. Daniel.

Much of this was new to Matthew, so he listened intently as they talked about the house. Finally, Mr. Daniel smacked his lips and turned to Matthew. "You should know that we are moving to another country."

* * *

Ms. Hopkins knocked on Terry's office door. She entered and stood by the doorway awkwardly. "I am so sorry about my sister. Ms. Teach fooled us all for a while. I might have been able to confront her and take her down, but I—"

"No!" interrupted Terry, "I'm the one who owes you an apology. I could have sent guards to take care of Hornet when I had the chance, but I let him escape. Now Hornet is hiding in the shadows and letting his army take over the battlefield."

Ms. Hopkins nodded. "I know you must be feeling sad about Hornet, Terry."

Terry let out a long breath. "I am supposed to be the brave one, leading people to victory. But right now, I feel it is working the opposite way. Hornet wants to scare me. He wants to take me down, and then destroy Angora. But we have hope!"

"What is it?" asked Ms. Hopkins, though she knew.

"The hope that Matthew comes back," said Terry, his voice quivering.

* * *

Isabelle was waiting at the port of Manta in Ecuador. "When will they be here," she wondered. Then, she noticed a huge yacht approaching and on top of it were Hornet, Melissa, Adam, and Alissa. She didn't recognize anyone except Hornet and shrugged at their appearance. Perhaps they were Hornet's friends. It took another minute for them to dock at the port.

"Everyone, meet Isabelle. Melissa, this is your older sister. Alissa, I'm reuniting you with your daughter who you haven't seen in many years," said Hornet.

All three stood speechless as Hornet looked at them. "I know this might come as shock since I took Isabelle with me when I left home so many years ago. I took care of her as you can see. It wasn't the right time for us to come together as a family. But we *are* family, and we must move on together."

Adam stood awkwardly next to them, a blank expression on his face. Hornet had cast a spell on him so while he could hear everything, he couldn't speak.

Alissa reached out to hold Isabelle's hand and had tears streaming down her face. Isabelle looked surprised and pushed Alissa's hand away.

Hornet continued speaking. "I know we have a lot to catch up on. I have already arranged everything. We will have a secure house to stay in and can plan out our next steps."

Little did they know, there was one other person interested in their conversation. Goliath stood at a distance behind a tree and was watching the scene carefully. She was relieved and happy to see Adam unharmed, although she thought he looked a little sick. While Hornet was making the introductions, she looked straight at Adam, willing him to look up. Just then, he raised his eyes and saw her. He smiled but put his fingers to his lips and shook his head.

Goliath understood. She had to follow them quietly. But now that she had seen Adam, she wasn't going to let him out of her sight.

* * *

Matthew was devastated. "What?! I understand that we need a new home but moving to another country? That is a completely different story!"

Mr. Daniel sighed. "Matthew, things have changed. Almost everybody who lives here works at the Jack Company. It will be too easy for Jack to find us, and I don't know what he will want from me. Also, you are going to have a baby brother very soon! Your mother needs to relax. We are going to leave Ireland and make a home for ourselves somewhere new," Mr. Daniel explained.

Matthew sniffled. "What is the point in moving. Jack has a global network. If he really wants to track us down, he can. If we stay here, we can show him we aren't scared and enough of our friends will support us. And what about me? What if Principal Terry can't track me and I never make it back to Magic World. How will I get to

Angora?"

Mr. and Mrs. Daniel glanced at each other. "Matthew, I am sorry, but you will also have to drop magic. Your magic skills are getting in the way of your academics, and, more importantly, your safety. If anyone sees you doing magic, we'll be reported to Jack immediately and be in prison or get killed. We need to protect our identity as much as we can and try to act like normal citizens," said Mr. Daniel.

Matthew's eyes started to grow wide, and he shook his head in disbelief. "Let go of Angora? I just saw magic. I made a...magical discovery."

Saying these last two words, Matthew felt his body begin to quiver. Mr. Daniel gave him a sympathetic smile. "I know you have made a magical discovery. But the thing is, Angora doesn't think of you as a magical discovery. Even in Magic World, some may think of you as a monster, an outsider," said Mr. Daniel.

Matthew took a deep breath. He didn't want to fight with his parents so soon after reuniting with them. "I have a lot to think about. I need to be on my own for a while," he said quietly as walked to the backyard. He lay down in the grass, thinking of what his mom and dad had just said. He didn't agree with them at all. Matthew had to know magic; they would be safe in Ireland; and nobody thought of him as a monster.

He picked a few blades of grass and spoke aloud: "Ireland, you will always be my home." He squeezed the green grass in his hand. "But life gives us more than one option. And I have already chosen my path, up there," he stated as he pointed to the sky. He saw the sun and thought it was beckoning him and he felt the breeze of the hot summer air, with Mother Nature surrounding him.

"This is what I like to see. It is what the Magic World teaches me to see." Matthew looked up and thought he saw a tiny orb, and on it, the letter **M**. "Notice things you would not expect," he added and looked back down at the grass and smiled at it, as though it was his best friend.

Made in the USA
Columbia, SC
24 February 2022

56346902R00143